One on One

Don Brand turned his back on everything in his life to play basketball. There was just nothing else he could do. He loved the game—the intricate moves and high-speed artistry of reflex and muscle.

But Killer Kane liked to play another kind of game on the court: the savage duel for which he'd been named. And he had a special reason for ending Brand's career...

BANTAM PATHFINDER EDITIONS

A comprehensive and fully integrated series designed to meet the expanding needs of the young adult reading audience and the growing demand among readers of all ages for paperback books of high quality.

Bantam Pathfinder Editions provide the best in fiction and nonfiction in a wide variety of subject areas. They include novels by classic and contemporary writers; vivid, accurate histories and biographies; authoritative works in the sciences; collections of short stories, plays and poetry.

Bantam Pathfinder Editions are carefully selected and approved. They are presented in a new and handsome format, durably bound and printed on specially selected high-quality paper.

PLAYOFF
BY WILLIAM COX

BANTAM PATHFINDER EDITIONS
TORONTO / NEW YORK / LONDON

A NATIONAL GENERAL COMPANY

RLI: $\dfrac{\text{VLM 7(VLR 4-7)}}{\text{IL 7-12}}$

PLAYOFF
A Bantam Pathfinder edition / published November 1972

*All rights reserved.
Copyright © 1972 by William R. Cox.
This book may not be reproduced in whole or in part, by
mimeograph or any other means, without permission.
For information address: Bantam Books, Inc.*

Library of Congress Cataloging in Publication Data

Cox, William Robert, 1901–
  Playoff.

  SUMMARY: Twenty-one-year-old Don cannot convince his father he is serious about basketball until he joins a professional team.

  [1. Basketball—Stories] I. Title.
PZ7.C83942Pl   [Fic]   72-7358

Published simultaneously in the United States and Canada

Bantam Books are published by Bantam Books, Inc., a National General company. Its trade-mark, consisting of the words "Bantam Books" and the portrayal of a bantam, is registered in the United States Patent Office and in other countries. Marca Registrada. Bantam Books, Inc., 666 Fifth Avenue, New York, N.Y. 10019.

PRINTED IN THE UNITED STATES OF AMERICA

PLAYOFF

1

Donald R. Brand, Jr. inserted the final piece of data into the maw of the huge computer and stood back, listening to its clacking, snapping, groaning mutter to make certain it was operating at peak efficiency. He reached for the basketball on the broad window sill behind him and absently bounced it, not looking at it, his extremely long fingers pronating, maintaining a tap-tap-tap that matched the smoothness of the magic machine of modern business.

A voice over the loudspeaker in the corner of the high-ceilinged room said, "Junior!"

He touched a switch and replied, "Yes, father?"

"Will you stop bouncing that confounded ball? Sanders can't concentrate with it banging in the room next to him."

"Yes, sir," said Donald R. Brand, Jr. He replaced the ball on the sill. He looked out across the cruelly manicured lawn of Technological Management Incorporated, past the gaunt bare flagpole toward the dreary traffic of the freeway beyond. He saw a bus turn off the exit ramp and crawl around the circle which led to the entrance of the stiffly modern stone-and-glass edifice in which he was confined. He watched, all else forgotten.

The bus stopped at the door of the gymnasium which Tech Management had paternally constructed for its employees. Giants disgorged. Donald Brand's hand went to the basketball; he picked it up as one would a grapefruit and caressed it, turning it in to rest against his hip.

He knew the big men, he had met them, he had watched them play basketball. There was Johnny Krash, the hard-nose, steady forward, and his running mate Charlie Mount towering six feet eleven inches. There was seven-foot Bud

Alcorn, the superstar center, who was an inch taller than his cousin Charlie Mount. There was the floor man, the brilliant Red Farber, and there was Killer Kane, the swaggering tough guy not limping from recent surgery but showing the marks of conflict on his battered face.

These were the Canyon City, California, Beavers. It was a club transferred from a megalopolis in the Midwest which would no longer support their huge salaries. These five were proven veterans, all stars. They were aging but they had a new coach and a new home and maybe new life.

They had come to play Tech Management's amateur industrial league team at Donald's invitation. It was, he believed, the only meaningful accomplishment he had achieved since he had graduated from college and come to work for his father's company. At least it was the only one meaningful to him.

The door to his oversized cell opened and Kitty McCoy came in and stood beside him. She was not a small girl, and her head came above his shoulder. She had auburn hair which fell long about her and brown eyes and a freckle or two. She wore little makeup but her blouse was form-fitting and her skirt well above shapely knees. She was altogether a lovely creature.

She said, "Still looking and longing, Junior?"

"Don't call me 'Junior,'" he snapped.

"Your father calls you 'Junior.' Your mother calls you 'Junior.' Why shouldn't I call you . . ."

"Just shut up," he said. He did not look at her. "I don't need any static from you, girl."

"I don't see why you're so unhappy. You get to play with the big boys this afternoon. You should be overjoyed."

"Oh, I'm ecstatic," he said. "I'm falling down with pleasure." Now he looked at her. "Did you have a dandy time with Homer Sanders last night?"

"We went to the Now Then," she said. "It was groovy."

"I'll just bet. All that great music. And so loud."

"You just don't dig discotheques," she said. "You are a jockstrap."

"I'm a damn junior engineer!" he shouted at her. "That's

what I am. I feed a stupid computer. A dumb, insatiable machine which sits there and smirks at me."

"Which is owned by the company in which your father holds not only a high position but a block of stock. Poor little you."

"Ain't it grand?" He snarled at her. "I also get to go out with you once a month. My father's secretary. *Executive* secretary, for gosh sake. Makes more money than I do. A real big career woman."

"Like I say, you're so lucky," she cooed. "I predict a great future for you. Business, maybe politics. Handsome young engineer runs for mayor of Canyon City. Whoopee."

"Will you knock it off?" He walked to the end of the computer and ripped out the card with the required solution punched into it.

"Well, you are papa's pride and joy," she said. "What papa wants, papa gets."

"So what?" His head was down, his brow rumpled.

"So fine. Great. Only you shouldn't cry about it. And you should quit playing with that basketball."

"And take up golf like Sanders? Cow-pasture pool at the country club, courtesy of good old Management Tech? Wriggling on the floor of the Now Then, that popular hangout for suburbanite youth?"

"One thing or the other," she said sweetly. "You're trying to eat your cake and have it too and that ain't done with any degree of ease."

"I happen to prefer basketball. You go the other route."

"And never the twain shall meet." She regarded him soberly, dropping her chafing manner. "You know, Don, if you'd wake up you might be a real nice kid."

"Kid? Kid? I'm twenty-one. I'm a year older than you are."

"Six months," she corrected him. "I'm twenty-one, also. But I know who I am."

"Oh, sure. You got yourself together. You're with it. Let it all hang out. Today's woman. You know what? Sanders is just right for you. He's the one'll be vice-president, the politician, all that jazz. He's really father's pet boy. Why don't you run in and cool it with him for a while?"

He grabbed the basketball and started for the door.

She said, "You forgot your card. And I forgot to tell you that your father wants to see you before you go down to the gym. Right on, Junior."

He glared at her, put the card in his pocket, and fled from the room. She could make him miserable at will and she often had the will to do so. He could never get the best of her. He would have hated her guts except for the fact that he was half in love with her.

He had known her since high-school days. They had been neighbors in Westwood until her father had died leaving not enough money for the family to continue in that neighborhood. At that time they had been sweethearts but she had entered UCLA and he had gone, perforce, to Cal Tech to endeavor to follow in his father's footsteps.

He had wanted to go to UCLA for the basketball but this had not been allowed. His mother had been dead since he was ten years old and his life had been completely dominated by his dynamic male parent. He had lost track of Kitty until she had reappeared at Management Tech, a brilliant, most efficient young lady of whom his father heartily approved—for Sanders or someone like him. Not for Junior, who was destined for higher things in the world.

Now he was twenty-one and his father had summoned him and he was well aware of the reason. There would be the same old lecture: basketball was a game; life was serious; the hours bouncing a rubber ball were wasted; he could have gained a master's degree if he had properly employed that time. It would all be delivered in the reasonable, even affable tone that his father took with him, the only child.

Well, he had spent the hours, all right. He paused at the door of the office next to his cubicle and stared at Homer Sanders, who was poring over a sheet of complicated theorems.

Sanders was a tall, wide man, a country-club athlete. He had thinning hair but his scalp was tanned as a coconut. Donald entered and deposited the card from the computer on the desk.

Sanders said, "Got it, eh, Donald? Just what I need to complete this problem. That is, if you fed it the proper data." He laughed, showing white, even teeth.

"Yeah, if I did. Coming to the game, Homer?"

"I doubt it. This is a must job, you know. Somebody has to finish it up."

"Better you than me. How was the Now Then last night?"

"I didn't have this problem yesterday," said Sanders stiffly. "I only got hold of it today."

"Oh, I didn't know. I thought you had it just before closing time yesterday," said Donald with assumed innocence.

"Well . . . it was quitting time." Sanders squirmed.

"And you had a date with Kitty McCoy. You know, Homer, I don't mind you being a pain in the butt. It's when you also want to be the saint in mod garments that you grab me where I get a pain." Donald turned on his heel and went down the corridor to the door leading to the office of his father, the superintendent of the plant, the Big Boss.

Outside the reception room he paused looking down at the basketball still in his hands. "Junior" was the key word that had set him off. He had always been "Junior." He was the kid who played basketball, a frivolous pursuit. He was the son of the scientist-businessman who was known throughout the world, a man decorated by the President for his contribution to the space age.

Kitty McCoy had started him on his rare inner rebellion. Homer Sanders had pushed him along. At this moment they represented all that he resented in his life thus far. Now he had to face his logical, reasonable father whom he had never been able to controvert. He was ill prepared. He knew what he wanted but he had no hope in the world of achieving his desire.

He drew a deep breath and entered the small, paneled, sparsely furnished waiting room. The girl receptionist smiled at him.

Her name was Martha Hall and she was small and dark and young. She was one person who did not make him feel callow, uncomfortable. She wore her hair short and her eyes were warm and interested. She was altogether feminine.

She said, "Good morning, Mr. Donald."

"Good morning, Miss Martha." He rolled the basketball on the cleared surface of her desk. "File this, please, before it attracts too much attention."

She picked off the ball in her tiny hands and gently placed it in her wastebasket. "He has someone in there."

Donald glared at the closed door. "He knows I want to get down to the gym."

"I know." She was all quick sympathy. "I'm really looking forward to seeing you play against the Beavers."

"They could kill me," he said moodily. "They won't because I'm the host. But they could."

"Oh, no they couldn't. You're good, real good."

"Thank you very much, Miss Martha."

"You're welcome, Mr. Donald," she said with dignity. "But you forget I know about basketball."

This was the truth. Martha's father and three brothers had been players and she was brought up in the atmosphere of the game. All the Halls were buffs. They dealt in the inside of the basketball lore and practice, and they knew all the moves and why they were made.

"You're also prejudiced." He grinned at her. She made him feel comfortably adult by her earnest manner.

"And you don't know who's in there talking to your father, either," she said.

"The King of Siam?"

"Mr. Hobie Reed, that's who."

"Reed? Now what in the world would he be talking to father about?"

"Maybe about you."

"Maybe you're really freaked out."

"I know Mr. Reed attended two of our games. You scored thirty-two points in each. You stole the ball six times. You had twenty-one rebounds."

"Against amateurs." Donald looked puzzled. "He saw the games? How do you know?"

"Papa invited him." She beamed. "He had his eye on you. There's trouble on the Beavers, you know that."

"Old age is all," said Donald, but his mind was whirling.

"Just the best bunch of veterans in basketball. Of course, Kane has to recover from his surgery."

"Or be dealt off," said Martha Hall.

"Now you're being squirrelly. Deal off Killer? He came with the franchise."

"He was the best guard in the world," she said. "But he's twenty-nine and hurting."

"He's next youngest to Johnny Krash on the starting five," said Donald. "He's forever."

The buzzer sounded and they both started at its demanding note. Donald said, "See you later, Miss Martha."

"Yes, Mr. Donald." She also had dimples and a twinkle in her round eyes. Her assumed respect was amusing—she always played the little game of "Mr." and "Miss" with solemnity. She made him feel good the few times they were together.

He paused and said to her, "Say, after the game . . . how about a bite to eat or something?"

"Gee, that wouldn't be right, would it, Mr. Donald?"

"Why not?"

"Well . . . you know how your father is about everything."

He said, "Uh, yeah. I know how he is."

He went through the door to the inner sanctum, scowling with the thought of how everything was. His father smiled from behind the desk—he was a medium-sized man who never stood in his son's company if he could avoid it.

"Donald. You know Mr. Reed, of course."

Hobie Reed was an aging giant who had been an all-pro basketball hero in another day and time. He held out a hand.

"How are you, Don?"

"Fine." He shook hands with the general manager and coach of the Canyon City Beavers. "How's the team?"

"We were just talking about it," said Reed. He looked at Donald Brand, Sr. and shook his head. "I'm sorry you don't agree with me, sir."

"Agree on what?" demanded Donald.

"Mr. Reed paid you a compliment. At least I know you will think it is a huge compliment."

"I'd like to hear it from him." Donald did not sit down.

"Well, I've been watching you. Scouting you, to tell the truth. A mutual friend suggested it. Man named Hall."

"Yes, I know Pat Hall."

"His daughter, I believe, is my receptionist," said Brand, Sr. dryly. "You may have noticed her on the way in."

"Pretty girl," said Reed. "As I say, I took a look. Liked what I saw. I thought maybe you'd like to have a sabbatical from business. We need youth right now. I have another deal in the making—can't talk about that right now. But you've got good hands, Don. And you're quick. Mostly that's what we want, speed and the hands. I'm sorry it can't be discussed."

"It's out of the question," said Brand, Sr. "Junior's future is here. Nice of you and all that."

Donald said, "You don't mean that you'd sign me to play with the Beavers? Me?"

"Why not? We wouldn't offer you a big bonus or anything like that. But we could give you a chance."

"The season opens in a week."

"I know it's rather late. There are matters—well, no use discussing all that. We appreciate the chance to work out with your guys this afternoon."

"Now, wait a minute," Donald said. It was all coming together inside him. He looked at his father. "You refused the offer for me, did you?"

"Of course. We decided all that when you did not attend a basketball school," said Brand, Sr. "Years ago we made the choice, didn't we?"

"Not we," said Donald. "You made the choice."

"I think we agreed."

"I was seventeen—no sixteen. I never did listen to anyone but you. I never have."

"And you're right," said his father, smiling. "You belong here, with the company, learning the ropes."

"I do?"

"Of course."

"But the company doesn't need me. Right?"

"Need you?" Brand, Sr. was incredulous. "Why, Junior, it'll be years before you are worth anything to the company. That's the very reason you must stick with the job."

Donald turned to Reed. "You heard him. They don't need me. I'm just Junior, the boss's son, you see?"

"Well, I wouldn't want to get into that," said the coach.

"I want to get into it. I want to get with it," Donald said. "The Beavers may not need me, but I'd be of some use or you wouldn't be talking to us. Right?"

"Right," said Reed.

"Now, Junior . . ."

Donald interrupted his father for the first time in his life. "I said I want to play basketball with the Beavers. Or at least try out. Is that plain enough, father?"

Brand, Sr. did not alter his smile. He tilted his head to one side and said agreeably, "Yes. Go on, Junior."

Donald gulped. The enormity of what he had just done overwhelmed him. Confusion clouded his mind, impeded his speech. Rebellion was new to him. It was not his natural role. He had been conditioned to accept the wisdom of his father.

He was aware that Hobie Reed was regarding him with interest and without enthusiasm. He knew he should continue to declare himself. He wanted to speak up. Inside him was a person with whom he was not familiar. He could not bring this new young man out into the open. He choked.

Brand, Sr. said in his gentle, logical fashion, "You see, Junior, you do not really want to desert the company. Basketball is a game. Well, a profession, if one accepts money for participating. But wouldn't the fact of a stipend tarnish the fun of playing the game? I believe it would."

Hobie Reed said heavily, "Yeah, well . . . It was just a notion. I better get back to the team. Nice to talk to you-all people."

He waved a hand and left the office. Donald, tongue-tied, stood hapless, helpless before his father. The inner man, the new man, seethed with anger and disappointment, trying to squirm his way out now that it was too late. He knew Hobie Reed had lost interest in him and he knew why: desire was the key to the game, any game. Donald had not shown enough desire to defy authority.

His father said, "We are very fortunate here, you know. Due to the cutback in NASA, and the slump in airplane manufacture, most of the other companies had to lay off help, reduce overhead. Because of our peculiar expertise in certain fields we are booming, burgeoning. Our future is secure. We intend to diversify, enter other fields in order that we maintain our strong position. I will discuss these matters with you at another time. I think the workday is ended, and Junior, please enjoy your basketball."

Donald opened his mouth to protest. He heard himself say, "Thank you, father."

Brand, Sr. smiled his serene smile and returned his attention to a single sheet of paper upon his Spartan-clean desk. Donald removed himself from the inner office.

Martha Hall beamed upon him, handing over the basketball. "See you after the game, Mr. Donald?"

"Uh . . . what?" He shook his head to clear away the fog. "Oh . . . yes?"

"You know what? I've never been to the Now Then." She dimpled at him.

"The . . . oh, sure. The Now Then. Yeah . . . well . . . later, huh?"

The pleased expression faded from her pretty face. "If you've changed your mind . . . or anything. I mean, if your father has other plans . . ."

"No," he said. "It's all right . . . I mean, we'll have fun. See you after the game, right?"

"Well, if you're sure."

"I'm sure. I'm sure." He took the basketball out of the reception room. He did not dribble it down the hall as was his custom. He carried it downstairs and into the modern, airy, bright gymnasium which had been his pride and joy. The Beavers were on the court in their warm-up long jeans and jackets, resplendent in gold and white.

Hobie Reed was sitting on the lowest row of the spidery stands. He waved and said, "Any time, Don."

Indifferent was the word for Reed's attitude, Donald thought, nodding, going into the dressing room. There were nine tall men in the last stages of dressing for the game. His indulgent father had allowed Donald to recruit them from the California colleges. They were basketball players who had not quite made the pros and who had good scholastic records. They were useful to Tech Management in their fashion and they played a good, solid game, better than most industrial teams. Donald had coached them, and he was the captain and the playmaker. They were full of the contest to come against the Beavers—a happy bunch of guys, calling out to him, cheerful, bright.

He tried to come up to the spirit of the occasion. He dressed and talked with them, telling them to play their game, stress defense, refuse to take bad shots, all the things he was expected to say. All the time the man within him was raging, kicking, scratching in an attempt to get loose.

He stamped into his Keds and stood. The team waited with respect for his final words. He licked dry lips. Then he said, "All right. Johnson, Bradbury, Murphy, Thompson. That's for starters. Everyone will play. We'll run. It's the only way we have a chance to stay with them. Run, double-team on the man with the ball. They're not kids, you know. We're younger and faster." He paused. Then he said, "Don't be overwhelmed by them. They're human and some of them are hurt. Let's make a showing against them."

Johnson, a black man almost seven feet tall, said, "Hey, Don. Should we whip 'em?"

There was a murmur of amusement. Donald swallowed. He did not smile. He said sharply, "Why not?"

Bradbury yipped. "That's the way to go. Right on! Let's get 'em."

They went piling out as though to a regular league game. Donald followed more slowly, his mind still awhirl. Martha was on the end of a row in the stands, waving to him. He saw Kitty McCoy's long legs and next to her Homer Sanders.

It was Kitty who had started it all. Then the smug Sanders and his lofty attitude had pushed it along. He had been rolling—until his father had sweetly reasoned for him.

Not with him.

For him.

The team began to warm up. Donald found himself going to where Hobie Reed sat apart.

"Hobie?"

"Yes, Don?"

"I'm going to ask a favor." He fumbled for words, then blurted, "No I'm not. I'm going to tell you something."

"Okay, shoot." Reed smiled without interest.

"I'm going to go in there and show you something." Donald's voice was deep in his throat, scarcely recognizable.

Hobie's eyes opened wide. "Something bothering you?"

"Everything. Every damn thing. My father . . . well, I've never been able to get past his logic. I know it. I'm not a clever talker. I'm not really a clever engineer. But let me tell you, I'm a hell of a basketball player."

"That's what I thought."

"Okay. And you thought I didn't care enough about it."

"Well, Don, after all. You didn't exactly show me."

A shadow fell across them. Donald didn't notice. "Right. I didn't. But I'm going to show you tonight. Right now."

A harsh voice said, "You're going to show us what?"

Donald turned. Killer Kane was staring at him. The veteran was six feet five, two inches taller than Donald. He was built proportionately, unlike many basketball stars. Only his hands were different, long, prehensile, opening and closing as if he exercised them every moment of time. His nose had been broken several times, and his brows bore the scars of elbows slung in close-contact play. There were deep lines in parenthesis from his nostrils past his hard mouth almost to his chin.

Donald said, "I wasn't speaking to you, Kane."

"No kidding? The rich kid don't talk to us slaves, huh?"

Reed said, "Butt out, Killer. This is private."

"Don't tell me where to go, coach," said Kane. "I've had it with you, too."

"You could say that again." Reed's face had darkened. He spoke to Donald. "Okay. You do what you can. We'll see."

"You'll see." Killer's face was made for sneering.

"You'll see nothing. These amateurs got a nerve goin' on the court with pros. Look out you don't get hurt out there, sonny."

"Donald. Don Brand." His voice matched the coldness of the veteran Beaver. "At least we don't cry over nothing."

"I'll show you cry. I'll show you a lot, rich kid."

"If you get to play," Donald said. "I hear you're hurting. Or is that an act to get your own way?"

"Why, you . . ." Kane pulled back a fist.

Reed was up and between them. He said, "That's enough. You want to fight? Do it on the court. Unless you want to rest up some more, Kane."

It was true, then, Donald was thinking. Martha had the right information. The superstar of yesterday and the coach were at loggerheads. He felt a surge of pleasure. He had no sympathy for Kane, who was a known bully, a big mouth, one of those who bragged and then proved he could do it all, a man disliked by many of the basketball world.

Kane was saying, "I wouldn't miss. Watch yourself, rich boy. I'll be there."

Reed said, "Anything out of line and you'll be fined, Kane, you better know that."

"Who needs to get out of line?" Kane laughed loudly.

Donald nodded to Reed and went onto the court to warm up. He took his time, working up a sweat, running in the circle with the others of the Tech team, shooting in his turn. He was somewhat amazed at himself but on the other hand he was terrifically pleased. It had taken years to struggle up and out of his shell. He had enjoyed it from the first moment.

The officials, hired by Tech Management, first-rate men, appeared in their black-and-white striped shirts. Donald spoke to them, introduced them to the scorekeepers—who were math experts from the company. The stands were filling with the few hundred employees of the company who were interested—the brainy types were not sports enthusiasts as a general rule. Donald looked up at Kitty and her lovely legs and her companion in his tweeds. She lifted a languid hand. He nodded without expression.

Martha Hall had been joined by her father, a privileged person, the only outsider allowed to come to the game. Donald went to where they sat.

"Hey, Pat. Who's that ugly kid with you?"

"Can I help it if her mother isn't as good-looking as I am?" Pat Hall was a six-footer, still youthful, red-haired. "What's with you and Hobie Reed?"

"You should ask." Donald was highly elated, the adrenaline was running strong. He had never felt quite this way, he knew. "We're going at 'em."

"I told him you would." Pat looked closely at Donald. "Hey, you're high as a kite. Cool it, man, cool it."

"Yeah." But he could not cool it. "Hey, thanks a lot for speaking to Hobie."

"I didn't think you'd mind. Your papa—that's another matter. How about him?"

"I'll tell you later," said Donald. He waved a hand and went to the bench where his team was gathering, the starters removing their sweat suits. He had always felt close to Pat Hall since his high-school basketball days. The big Irisher was a competitor and a sound basketball man. He was in the real-estate business with his sons, and found time to retain his interest and affiliations.

He had taken the Halls for granted, Donald realized. His one contribution had been to recommend Martha to his father for her job as receptionist. It was time, he thought, to count his friends, his real friends.

The squad gathered around him and he said, "One last thing. Remember we agreed to play pro rules. They'll put hands on you. They'll charge if you block. You've seen enough of their play. Get right at 'em—they won't be expecting it."

The referee blew a whistle. Donald slapped hands with the team and ran out on the floor. The Beavers strolled into position, relaxed, the big boys playing with children. Johnson of Tech faced off against Bud Alcorn who reached out a hand, then grinning, touching the top of Johnson's head, indicated that they were exactly equal in height.

Hobie Reed started his regulars, Krash and Mount at the forwards, Farber and Killer Kane at the guards. They were all smiling, agreeable, touching flesh in the time-honored fashion, except Kane. He gave Donald a deadly glare and turned his back. The pros were a formidable sight, all but Alcorn taller and heavier and more experienced in every movement.

The referee put the ball in the air and the battle was on. Johnson was a good jumper but Alcorn seemed to ascend as from a trampoline. The Beaver center flicked the ball back toward Killer Kane, the playmaker.

Kane reached for the ball without looking, watching for the development downcourt. The Beavers were forming for offense with the Techs closely guarding. Kane paused a moment, dribbling.

Donald Brand flew into action. Everything left his mind now excepting the problem at hand. He snatched, leaning, thrusting. Kane never saw him.

Donald cleanly clapped away the ball. He followed it to the sideline and began dribbling. Kane, startled, went into hot pursuit.

Donald ran clean away. He swept down to the basket and made his layup unmolested. The first two points went to the despised amateurs of Tech.

A yell came from the stands where Martha and Pat Hall were seated. It was picked up a bit unevenly but with appreciation by some of the others. The Beavers came down to put the ball in play from under the Tech basket.

Every Tech man covered his opponent. They were young and swift and eager. First blood by Donald had given them the momentum, the lift all athletes know and recognize at once.

Kane passed out to Farber. The ball went back to Kane. The Beavers began a controlled, determined march down the boards.

The Techs covered as best they could. It was at once apparent that they did have the speed if not the skills. They ran all around the bigger, stronger Beavers. They harassed each player, waving arms high.

Kane made his famed move, trying to shake loose. He swerved out, then back. His knee gave a little, but he was still a fast and graceful big man.

Donald anticipated the break. He switched from Farber

and went into the path of a pass from Alcorn on the low post. Again Kane reached for the ball and again Donald was there first.

Spinning, holding the ball, Donald looked for Tommy Thompson. He found his fellow guard on the sideline and slammed the ball to him, then cut for the basket.

He found an elbow in his ribs. It shook him off stride. He saw Kane's hip coming at him as the officials watched Tommy make a hard pass to Johnson on the high post. He sidestepped. Again Kane threw the hurtful elbow.

Donald saw it coming. He chopped with his right hand, slamming knuckles into Kane's forearm. He sped past Kane. He went down into the pattern and Johnson passed to him. Thompson made his drive for the basket. Donald faked, then bounce-passed.

Tommy took the ball and went up for his jump shot. There was no opposition as the Beavers were caught flat-footed. The ball swished through the net and the Techs had four points to nought for the pro Beavers.

Pat Hall's voice came loud and clear, "Attaway to go, men. Take it to 'em!"

The Beavers brought the ball back down the court. Farber and Kane passed back and forth. Alcorn assumed the low post. Johnson stayed with him. Alcorn made a move, got the ball. Johnson was fooled and Alcorn went for the basket. Johnson blocked him and it was a foul cleverly engineered by the big Beaver center, a pro ploy.

Alcorn made the free throw to give the Beavers their first score. He missed the second one and Johnson went high to gather it off the board.

Thompson put the ball into play. Donald began to dribble for the basket. Kane, defending, pressed close, going backward as Donald went forward. Knowing that Kane's knee was not fully healed Donald feinted, then turned on the speed. He saw Bradbury in the clear and passed off. Before he could get started again Kane had him by the belt, holding him, throwing him off stride, concealing the foul by staying so close the officials could not get a good look.

Donald stopped dead. Kane came even with him. Donald twisted loose. Kane stumbled and Donald used his elbow.

Kane winced with pain and yelled for a foul. The officials were intent on the play action and paid him no heed.

Donald said, "Why don't you grow up, Killer? Play ball and knock off this kid stuff."

Kane said, "I'll show you kid stuff."

Alcorn was blocking a try by Thompson. Bradbury went up and the ball bounded off the iron into his hands. Farber guarded Bradbury as Donald ran down to help on the play. Kane deliberately kicked Donald in the ankle.

Donald went down. An official blew his whistle and indicated the foul, then went to Kane and shook a finger at him, threatening to throw him out of the game.

Donald regained his breath and said, "Leave him in there. I'll take care of him."

He went to the foul line. There was a hot ball of fire in his middle. He had never been so angry on or off the basketball court. For a moment he was shaky, then he grew coldly confident as the fire diminished to a steady glow. He sank his foul. He turned and looked for Killer Kane.

The rough pro was there with bells on. He dogged Donald's every step. He was as sticky as glue. The other eight men played the game, but these two fought a duel. It was, Donald thought, bad basketball but he had no other choice than to meet the challenge. He found himself a step faster. Kane's hands were as quick as those of anyone but his knee hampered him. They battled up and down the boards until Thompson, double-teamed, desperately passed to Donald.

Kane covered him like a blanket, working close, one hand on him, one arm waving in his eyes. Farber came over to help.

Donald spun, dribbled behind his back. Both men against him were slightly off balance. Donald made his favorite swift sidestep. Alcorn loomed on the low post.

Donald bent low, passed between the long legs of Alcorn. It was a daring move but he had seen Bradbury cutting for the basket.

Bradbury took the pass and was clear. He set for a split second, then put the ball through the hoop.

Kane ran into Donald from behind, pretending to stumble. His fist went into Donald's kidneys.

From the bench Hobie Reed called time out. Donald took his team to the bench, glancing over at the Beavers. Reed was standing tall, speaking to Kane. The Killer waved his arms. Reed made a gesture.

Kane stood a moment. It seemed he was about to swing a punch at Reed. Then he grabbed his warm-up clothes and stalked across the court to the dressing room.

"Martha must have been one hundred per cent correct," said Donald.

"What was that? What's the matter with Killer?" Johnson asked. "He crazy or something?"

"I think he's through as a Beaver," Donald said. "Look, you guys are doing great. We're leading them. From now on look out. They'll get it together. Just play your game. We'll start substituting when they do, no big deal, just a good workout for us. Okay?"

"I'm so proud of us now I could bust," said Johnson. "We've already showed them we're no pushovers."

Time was resumed and they went onto the court. The guard who replaced Killer Kane was Peanuts Hopwood, a veteran in his early thirties, a strong, amazingly swift black man with a grin that never came off his mobile features.

Hopwood said, "Hey, man, Killer was right on you."

Donald said, "It was mutual. But it wasn't basketball."

"Let's you and me play," said Hopwood.

They proceeded to do just that. Hopwood had more moves than a checker champion playing four opponents at once. He was about the same size and build as Donald; it was a good match-up but the veteran knew all there was to know.

Furthermore the Beavers picked up a flow with Hopwood on the court. They began to play like the experienced team they were. It was a complete turnabout.

The quarter ended with the Beavers ahead, twenty-five to sixteen. Donald wiped his face on a towel and eyed his teammates.

"Now we know."

"You can bet on that," said Johnson.

Thompson said, "I can't get loose for a shot. And when

I think I'm ready there's a jumping jack between me and the basket."

"We're younger," Donald said. "Keep going. Jake, you and Ostrander come in for a while. Brad and Tommy take a rest and watch the action. Maybe we'll learn a way."

They went back on the court. For five minutes it was all the Beavers. They scored eight in a row. Then Donald found himself getting free. Hopwood's age was telling on him. He tried to slow down the action. It was only split seconds but it made a difference.

Donald tried one from twenty feet out. It went in. He intercepted a pass. He tossed to Murphy, who got to Johnson on the high post and Alcorn could not prevent the Tech center from dipping one through the net.

Tommy and Bradbury came back on, fresh and eager. The teams traded baskets. At the half it was fifty for the Beavers, forty for the home team. Pat Hall was cheering as though it were a victory.

In the dressing room Donald said, "They are slower. It's amazing but I see now . . . " He broke off. He was thinking about Hobie Reed's comments. There was now a growing excitement which sent the blood coursing through his arteries.

Johnson said, "You were right, Don. We just use our speed and stay in the game. If we come within thirty of them it'll be something, right?"

"They've beaten the top teams by more than thirty. But not lately," Donald said.

"What's with Kane? You got an idea?"

"Yes. I have a big notion. Let's just go back and keep on playing fast and tough." He washed his hands and face. He was in top condition—he did not feel tired. He had never been out of shape, he thought, for no good reason except that he loved basketball and wanted always to be ready to play. He had never felt more ready than he did at this minute. He was under no illusions about the Beavers. They had not hit their peak, they were consummate pros, but tonight he had no feeling that they were so many miles ahead of him.

The teams took the court. Kitty McCoy still sat with Homer Sanders. She waved at Donald. Martha and Pat

Hall yelled encouragement and he blew them a kiss, grinning, bowing. The teams went onto the court.

Peanuts Hopwood slapped hands with Donald and said, "Hey, man, you swing pretty good."

"Not as good as you."

"Got to learn." The wide grin lessened. "Then just when you get it all together Old Man Time catches up."

"You do all right," said Donald. "You do fine."

Peanuts chuckled. "Show you a trick or two, huh, boy?"

"Right on," said Donald.

Refeshed by the halftime period the Beavers got the tip and started a dazzling attack downcourt. It was here they could run away and hide, Donald knew. He switched from Peanuts Hopwood as the play developed. He helped Thompson double-guard Farber. He saw an opening, sneaked in low and used his quick hand to slap at the ball. He knocked it loose.

He was on it in a moment. He had to dribble to allow the Techs to get down to their basket. Peanuts came at him. He switched hands, gave Hopwood his hip and backed around. He spun, saw Johnson on the low post and flung the ball high. Johnson leaped to catch it.

Donald ducked and ran. He got to the corner. Johnson passed to the other side, hitting Bradbury. Farber covered Bradbury and Donald broke inside. Bradbury gave him the ball. Donald flipped it through for two points.

Again the Beavers tried a fast break. The amateur Techs doggedly stayed with them. It was a standoff until Alcorn took the shot within the required twenty-four seconds. The big center hit for his field goal.

Now the Beavers had the momentum. They swept up and down and they scored from outside. Nothing could stop a professional scoring from outside, Donald thought. It was an avalanche. The score ran to seventy-two for the Beavers, forty-four for the Techs. The quarter ended and Pat Hall came to the Tech bench.

"Don't feel bad," he said. "You guys are playing up. Any other amateur team would've folded. Hang in there."

"They sure can go," said Donald wistfully. "How they can go."

"They must be tiring a bit," said Pat Hall. "Go at 'em."

They went back and went at them. Donald felt no weariness. He was all over the court. His teammates played their hearts out. They scored.

But Alcorn had the boards and Farber and Krash scored. Peanuts slowed down and seemed to saunter—always to the right spot. Donald whirled like a dervish to cause three turnovers from which the Techs scored but the Beavers were able to come right back. Poise and experience told the tale.

The final horn blew. The Beavers had scored one hundred. The Techs had managed seventy-five points. It was no disgrace but Donald wished it had not ended; he wished he could go on and on playing against these people.

Flushed, exalted, he shook hands with the Beavers, thanking each from the bottom of his heart. He had never been so thrilled in his life. He was at last out of that core, his own man. He floated off the floor.

When he came to the dressing room he abruptly sat down. For a moment or two he doubted that he would ever get up. Johnson lay on the rubbing table, his long legs dangling over the end. The others collapsed in various awkward positions. They were too weary to exchange conversation. One by one they straggled to the showers.

Johnson turned his head and said to Donald, "There's no way any team in the industrial league can beat us now. I got my doctorate out there tonight."

Then he went to the showers. Donald rubbed at his head with a towel. The door opened and Hobie Reed entered.

Donald managed to get to his feet and grin. "That was worth a lot. I can't thank you enough."

Reed was sober-faced. "Want to talk. Okay?"

"Sure, anything." He sat down again and Reed perched up on the table. "Shoot."

"I'm making that deal. I'm trading Kane for Beans Jordan."

"Beans Jordan? That whacked-out kid?"

"Yes. The million-dollar boy that couldn't make it with the Jaybirds. The all-time collegiate big head. I'm trading for trouble and I'm paying his salary."

"Hobie you have to be out of your skull."

"Maybe. On the other hand you saw what we have. Superstars—and they're old and tired. They've got guts and skill but no legs. Like Peanuts—five minutes of beauty and then you handled him."

"He's great, though."

"Not strong enough. Alcorn, Farber, Mount, Farrell, Krash—all over thirty. Felton is twenty-eight. Tip Harper's twenty-seven but they're not topflight, they're journeymen. You showed me tonight. You're better than my second string."

"No wait, Hobie. I was high tonight."

"You had the desire. You wanted to try yourself against the pros. You showed me enough. I can't pay you what you are probably worth. But I have to make the offer again. I want you."

"Money isn't it," Donald said. His heart was beating too fast. "It's . . . well, it's my father."

"I could see that. It's a question of what you want to do. It seemed to me that you wanted basketball. It seemed to me that you wanted to have your shot at the pro game. Well, maybe Pat Hall put it in my mind. When I watched, I saw that you had certain characteristics which make the star player. Raw, sure. Inexperienced. But you go all out. I need young guys who will do that, go all the way to win."

"Like Beans Jordan?"

"Beans will either come around or I'm a lousy coach. He's your age. I need two fast kids. He can shoot like the best gunner you ever laid eyes on. You can play defense and you don't shoot too bad. I have to rebuild right now, while the older guys can help teach by their example. I had to get rid of Killer Kane because he wouldn't be of help. I can pay you five thousand to sign and fifteen thousand with bonuses if we go to the playoffs. I know it's not much in these days but it's what I can do."

"It's not the money," Donald said again. A trumpet seemed to be blowing somewhere near at hand. His heart had resumed its normal beat but his mind was floating. The sound of the trumpet grew louder, more triumphant. He said, "Hobie, just a couple of hours ago I couldn't make a decision. The thought of defying father was overwhelming. It was beyond me. I started to talk and couldn't. Now . . . well . . . you've got a deal."

"It's a big step," said Reed. "Your father will be very unhappy with us both."

"Will he not?" Donald managed a laugh. "That's my problem. Like I say, I'm twenty-one. He's had his way up until now. It's time for me to grow up."

"I can count on you, then? I have to know. Time's growing short, and there's an awful lot to accomplish. If you back down I'll be on the spot."

"You have my word," said Donald. "Draw up a contract. I'll sign tomorrow."

Reed shoved out his hand. "I believe you. It's going to be tough but let's make it worthwhile."

It was a warm handclasp. Reed left to join his team. Donald went to the showers. He was half-dressed before he remembered he had a date with Martha Hall.

2

Northwest of Canyon City Don Brand turned his convertible off the freeway and drove up a hill atop which lights beckoned to the passerby with glittering fingers. Beside him Martha Hall was tiny and quiet. His thoughts were deep and restless, and he was just a bit frightened by the possible consequences of his act. He pulled into the parking lot of the Now Then and allowed a red-coated youth to take the car.

The Now Then was new, as all of Canyon City and environs were newly built, part of the population explosion of southern California. The ownership had created a complex of entertainment—a movie theater, a discotheque, two bars, a dining room for the country-club set—all segregated around a square containing a fountain, a garden, and park benches. The two young people walked arm in arm to the quieter section. Music from the discotheque drummed across the mall, there was laughter from one of the bars, and the façade of the theater advertised a French film.

Inside the room was large and dimly lighted with booths all around. There was a small dance floor and a five-piece muted band. A maître d' escorted them to a place removed from the band, spoke Don's name with respect, proffered gigantic menus.

Martha said, "Would you call it posh?"

"I never thought of it one way or the other," Don said.

"They know you."

"They know father." He twisted on the leather seat. "I know him, too. He'll be working at home tonight. I have to face him."

"Yes. You'll have to face him." Her voice was low and pleasant. "Aren't you starving?"

"I should be but I'm not."

The waiter stood by, pencil poised. "Shall I order?" she asked.

Don said, "Hey, I'm not that flaked out. How about a cocktail?"

"A martini, please."

"Two martinis, very dry. Steak okay, Martha?"

"Filet, please. Baked potato, salad with Roquefort and the green beans," she recited.

"The same." He was surprised at her poise. "You sure you want the athlete's dinner?"

"I have a father and three brothers, remember?"

He looked after the departing waiter. "Yeah. And I remember you're not yet twenty-one and shouldn't be served a drink."

"They're voting at eighteen," she said. "And I only take one. And who cares?"

"Not me," he said. "I'm a one-drink man myself. Like Kitty says, I'm just a jock."

"Kitty should know. She's a very smart lady."

"Too smart sometimes."

"She's sitting across the room, you know," Martha said.

He jerked around, staring, then wished he hadn't. Kitty raised a hand in her habitual fashion. Homer Sanders nodded. They were seated close together in the booth opposite Don and Martha. He waved back at them, regaining composure.

Martha said, "You've been going with her a long time, haven't you?"

"No. I've *known* her a long time."

"I see." She smiled a small smile. The cocktails arrived and she lifted her glass. "Here's to you and the Beavers."

"Thanks. Here's to you and your father."

"Dad not only knows basketball . . . he knows men."

"What does that mean?"

"He picked you."

His eyes strayed to Kitty without volition. "I never tried being a man before. Just 'Junior the jock.' It's new and oddlike."

"Maybe we should be over yonder doing our thing with the other young folks? In the discotheque?"

"Maybe we should." All the other diners were older people. All except Kitty McCoy. Even Homer was past thirty. "Only that never has been my thing."

"You sure do low-rate yourself, Don," she said. "Why?"

He sipped the cocktail, considering. "My father is that much more intelligent. My mother was a scientist too, you know. Everybody's so clever."

"Kitty, too?"

"Never mind Kitty."

"Touchy, too, aren't we?" Her voice was not so pleasant.

"Not really." The truth was that his new-found courage to face his father, to quit Technological Management Incorporated, and to brave the professional basketball world was oozing from him. Part of it might be the sight of Kitty out for the second night in a row with Homer Sanders, he knew. He finished the martini. The band struck up an old Gershwin tune in dance time and he said, "Let's stop yakking and dance, shall we?"

They joined other couples on the floor. He was too tall for her and he had never been a good dancer. They passed Kitty and Homer, smiling in the fashion of people on the dance floor, paying only half-attention. They went around twice and then Martha pulled away.

"Your mind's not on it, Don."

"My feet are not with it," he confessed.

They sat down in the booth. Kitty and Homer floated, perfectly matched. Don stared at the small girl across the table.

"I'm great company. The charm boy of the western world. Will you excuse me? I'm really sorry."

"You've made a big decision," she said. "It's not easy."

He sighed. "If you make a decision you should stick with it. I know all the rules."

"You'll stick."

The music stopped, leaving Kitty and Homer near the table. They stood arm in arm, smiling.

Kitty asked, "Having a good time, children?"

"Dandy," said Don.

"Lovely," said Martha. "You two make a lovely couple on the floor."

"Thank you, ma'am," said Homer in his country-club

way. "Hope you enjoy your dinner." He tugged Kitty away. They did not look back.

"She's punishing you for something," Martha said quietly. "Don't let her see that you're upset."

"Who's upset?" But he was dissimulating, he knew. He was glad that the steaks arrived just then.

They ate in silence. He noted her hands, incredibly small and deft and pretty. She was a good kid and the Halls were his friends. He felt guilty for not showing her a better time. As they finished the music started again. He called for the check and signed it.

He said, "Let's see how the other half lives."

"Like where?"

"Like where it's at."

"You really want to?"

"This is like a morgue."

She said brightly, "Okay, let's make the scene, man."

He managed to wave nonchalantly at Kitty as they departed. They walked across the parklike mall to where the sound of wild music slithered out on the air. This was another world.

Lights revolved kaleidoscopically—reflecting from mirrors in ceiling and walls. High up in a glass booth a pretty girl danced as she fed tape cassettes to the recorder. Amplifiers blasted the sound of electrified instruments. The beat was steady, the noise gaily terrific. Couples faced each other going through the motions of the freeform modern dance. There was the atmosphere of abandoned gaiety yet there was no touching, no coming together of bodies or hands.

Don said, "This I can handle."

"Handle it," she challenged.

They went into the throng, loose-jointed, facing each other with smiles. They felt the beat, the heavy, continuing rhythm of the music. They moved as they felt it, this way and that, knees bending, arms flying, turning, returning. They were a part of the dancers yet separated from them. They were compelled by the sound but not controlled by it.

For the first moment since he had realized the enormity of his handshake with Hobie Reed a feeling of peace and enjoyment permeated Don's psyche. The little girl danced to him, backed away, and he grinned down at her. Life seemed bright again.

A harsh voice cut into his euphoria. "Well, get him. The rich jock's got a broad."

He wheeled to face Killer Kane. A hard-faced girl with too much makeup seemed to be Kane's partner.

Don said, "Hello, Kane."

"Hello my left rear foot," said Kane. "A rich jerk is still a jerk to me. Outa my way."

It was evident that Kane had not stopped with one cocktail. The sharp elbow Don remembered well from the basketball court jabbed into his ribs—there was pain. Martha's face showed fright.

It all exploded. Don sidestepped, then seized a wrist and an elbow. He bent Kane's arm behind his back. He spun and doubled the man over. Kane bellowed with rage.

The dancers parted. Don turkey-walked Kane toward the door. The manager came on the run, recognized Don. The door opened magically. Don shoved Kane out into the night, shoved him away and waited.

Kane stumbled. He staggered a few steps. He fell backward into the pool formed by the waters of the fountain. A security officer appeared from the shadows.

"All right, Mr. Brand?"

The manager came and said swiftly, "The man was annoying people. Just get rid of him. No publicity, please."

"Yes, sir," said the officer, loosening a blackjack in his belt. "I'll handle it. Nice to see you, Mr. Brand."

Martha was waiting outside the door. They walked together to the parking lot and gave the youth the ticket. They waited for the car.

She said, "That was very nice, Don. No fuss, no muss."

"He's paranoiac," Don said. "I guess he's had so many injuries that his mind is affected. He's still a great athlete. One of the best who ever lived."

"You can't hate anyone, can you?" she asked softly. She was smiling up at him.

"What's to hate?" He was calm now. He had gone through one phase after another. He felt able, capable again, as he had during the game against the Beavers.

"One thing father tried to teach me: keep cool, face the problem, use your brains. Maybe I learned."

"You learned. If you'd hit him in there—riot time. You did what had to be done."

"You're pretty cool yourself."

"Like I said. Three brothers and an athletic dad. A girl gets so she knows the score."

They chatted all the way to her home across Canyon City, a sprawling house with a basketball court in the rear beside an Olympic swimming pool. He parked.

"Why do you work?" he asked. "You don't have to."

"I like it. I like your father."

"And Kitty?"

"Oh, Kitty's fair. Strict but honest. She's my boss, really, you know. She doesn't gig me."

"I don't work there any longer," he said wonderingly.

"I'll miss you and your basketball."

"I'll give it to you for a keepsake."

"I'll put it in my wastebasket."

He said, "I'm sorry it wasn't more fun tonight."

"Fun? I was having great fun when Killer butted in. And watching you take care of him was enough excitement for a couple of evenings."

She opened the door of the car and he hastened around to offer her a hand. She leaped out and paused. He held her hand.

She said, "Talk straight to your father, please?"

"Straight?"

"Let him know how you admire him. It'll be hard for him."

"I hadn't thought of that."

"Think of it." She gave his hand a squeeze and darted up the path to the house. He stood a moment looking after her. She was a very smart little girl. She was a friend he did not ever want to lose.

He recrossed the city and entered Grove Estates, went through a gate and proceeded under stately eucalyptus trees to the mansion his father had built. He put the convertible into a garage which held three other automobiles. He went through a door into an entryway and then to a hall. He walked down the hall to the door of his father's study and tapped.

"That you, Junior?"

He winced and entered. "Hello, father. Working as usual."

Brand, Sr. looked up from a legal pad full of hieroglyphs and smiled. "Habit, Junior, just a bad habit. Did you have a nice dinner?"

"Yes. I was with Martha Hall."

"Lovely girl. Very efficient. Quiet, too."

"Yes. A nice girl. Father, I've something to tell you."

"I thought as much."

"You're not going to like it."

"Am I not?" He was calm.

"No. You're not."

"Well?"

Don thought of Martha. He sat across the desk and looked at his father. He saw a rather small, greying but fresh-faced man of unquestioned intelligence.

"You're pretty great, you know. You've always been great. I'm the one who's not in line."

"In what way, Junior?"

"Well, you and mother . . . and everyone else around . . . brains. Genius. Me? I've just been 'Junior.' "

"You've done your best. You are slow in developing, which is no problem. You'll come into your own."

"I hope so. But not at Tech Management."

His father leaned forward and folded his hands on the desk before him. His eyes grew serious, somewhat sad. "I see. You've made up your mind."

"Yes."

"Basketball. Mr. Reed. The Beavers."

"Yes."

Mr. Brand leaned back and unfolded his hands. They looked curiously helpless, loosely open on the desk top. "You're very sure."

"I'm really very sure."

"The old sayings confront us. 'Never try to fit a square peg in a round hole.' "

"You've always tried to do what is best for me," said

Don. "I know that. I'm just not right for engineering. I am right for basketball."

"We could inaugurate a program here. You could act as coach," said Mr. Brand tentatively. "It would be better than going into the strain and stress of the professional game."

"One thing you have taught me, sir. Go for the top. The best. Never settle for less."

Mr. Brand nodded. He managed a smile. "You have me there. I don't like it, Junior. I'll never be reconciled to it. But I will discontinue to stand in your way."

"Thank you, father."

"I can't even wish you success. I would rather have you back in the company after you've had your chance and failed."

"That's all right."

"But I do wish you luck and pray you won't be injured." The hands turned over and picked up the papers.

"Yes, sir." Don got up and walked to the door. He turned around. "I'll keep in touch."

"Of course." Mr. Brand's eyes were on his work.

Don left the room, closing the door quietly behind him. His father put down the papers. He slumped in the chair. His chin sank upon his chest. He remained in this position for a full five minutes.

Then he reached into a drawer of his desk. He took out a book. The title was *Basketball Among the Pros*. He began to read.

The long, low Maserati growled past a truck-and-trailer rig at one hundred miles an hour, negotiated a long curve, and came to a divided road. One sign pointed to California. The other indicated that Nevada was to the east. The imported auto slowed only for a moment, then swung toward Nevada.

The driver was Oscar "Beans" Jordan. He was coming from Northwest City, home of the professional basketball team known as the Jaybirds. He was due at the training camp of the Canyon City Beavers. He snickered to himself, driving toward Las Vegas. It was a very simple choice for him. He had never seen Las Vegas, gambling capital of the world.

He was twenty-one years of age. He was six feet four inches tall. His hair was blond and hung almost to his collar. His collar was wide open. He wore mod pants, hip-snuggers striped black and red. In several banks he had deposited the money left from taxes, a lot of money. When he dropped out of the college at which he had been an All American the Jaybirds had bestowed upon him over a hundred thousand dollars.

That he had been traded for the aging, injured Killer Kane bothered him not a whit. He knew how good he was. He was the best shooter in the world. His opinion of the coach and the players of the Jaybirds was lower than their opinion of him.

Furthermore he worried not at all about joining the Beavers. They were, he figured, a bunch of old men who desperately needed a young, swift gunner. They had been tremendously clever in making the trade. Nothing could deter Beans Jordan from his march to the top. Nothing ever had . . .

It had not been always thus. He did not care to remember the beginnings. He did not want to think about his hillbilly beginnings, the family living in direst poverty, the underwear made from flour sacks. He did not want to remember his brutal, ignorant father nor his ailing mother who had died long since. He had sent home enough money to care for the brothers and sisters who knew no better than the hills, the hardscrabble farm, the local juke joints. They had never understood him nor cared for him.

They had tried to prevent him from going into town and attending the high school after he had found the old basketball and practiced with a peach basket nailed to a tree and learned that he had the gift. They were all runts, his father a stringy five-six. He had clobbered them good and then walked away. He had found people who would take care of him while he shot from everywhere on the floor and led his team to the national scholastic championship almost single-handed.

It had been the same in college. There were always folks who would pay his way. He had worked, true. He had worked at hard labor in the summer to build muscle. He had worked behind counters, charming the ladies, selling. But always he had known his destiny. All time All American, some had said. He paid no heed to those who criticized his defensive work on the floor. He was the king of gunners, and that was enough.

The money was fine, of course, but the money wasn't all-important in itself. What he loved was the great things money could buy. The car, the clothes, the good times, the beautiful chicks—they were the baubles he adored. Then of course there were the cheers of the crowd when he sank a long one. Maybe the cheers were most important.

Even in the Northwest, on a losing team, some had appreciated him. Blond hair flopping, running, spinning, making his famous moves he had scored again and again from the outside. With any support, he knew, he would have brought the Jaybirds into the playoffs with his skill.

Right now, on the road, he began to think about the Beavers and Canyon City. The team played its home games in an auditorium newly built halfway between the hometown and—Hollywood. He almost turned the car around when he thought of the movie town.

All his life he had huddled in dark theaters staring up at the silver screen. All his pleasure when he was in high school had been basketball and movies. The celluloid dreams had been his dreams. Now he was going to headquarters. Now he would meet the stars—there were dozens of sports fans among them, male and female, he had read in the sports magazines. He would actually meet them and they would admire him because he was Beans, the gunner, the beautiful shooter.

Of course he had been at Los Angeles before, playing with the Jaybirds. That was different, for he was an outlander, one of the opposition. They had not recognized him then. Now he would be a hometown boy.

It was too much. It was too groovy. Maybe he would get a chance to appear on television or in a picture. He was, after all, young and handsome. He could cut it with a little help. Coaching, training, whatever, he could perform—all he needed was a chance. He would quit basketball tomorrow if he could make it as an actor.

He sang a little hillbilly song as he drove the powerful automobile toward Las Vegas.

The house rested upon the plateau of a hill in a new and exclusive development between Canyon City and Bel Air. It was not an ordinary house. It had been built to order at great expense. The doors were all eight feet high. The ceilings were twelve feet from the floors. The furnishings were custom-made for a giant. People of normal size were dwarfed when they entered the luxurious quarters of Harold "Bud" Alcorn, superstar, center of the Canyon City Beavers.

He moved toward the outdoors, and the patio and pool which overlooked the valley. It was night and the lights shimmered and glittered like fireflies far below. He was wearing slacks and moccasins and a crew-neck shirt of light tan. His sensitive features were knitted as though he was smelling something not quite rotten but not ripe, either.

He sat down in a specially constructed folding lounge

chair and leaned back. The stars also twinkled at him. He received no particular message from them but he liked to watch them, to trace the constellations, to name them to himself.

He was interrupted by the sound of motor cars. He heard the men coming through the house led by his tall cousin Charlie Mount. They came out to him, Charlie and Peanuts Hopwood and Sam Felton and Tip Harper, all black men, all serious.

Bud Alcorn said, "Gentlemen."

"Hi, Bud," said cousin Charlie. "Wanted to talk to you."

"So you said." He did not arise. "Where's Johnny and Red and Farrell and Carey? Where's the new man, Jordan?"

"This is about us. Not them. Us."

"You say." Alcorn sat up straight. "This was supposed to be a team meeting."

"Bud, those cats don't dig," said Charlie Mount. "You're the captain. You're the big man. We only want to talk to you."

"About what? The team? Man, the team's not here."

"Not the team exactly. The way things are. Breed tradin' away Killer for that flake. Bringin' in the new guy from the amateurs. And the flake didn't even bother to report today."

"And what's that got to do with just you and me?" demanded Bud Alcorn.

"It's the whiteys," Sam Felton broke in. "The way they're managing. It's all wrong. If you were to speak up —well, they'd have to listen."

"You think so?"

"Man, they're paying you over a hundred and fifty grand a year. Without you the team's nothing."

"I've got a big message for you," said Alcorn. "With me the team's not much."

"But you could do something."

Alcorn reclined in the overlong lounge chair. "What you're saying is that the white man's letting you down."

"Us. You and all of us. The white players, too."

"But you didn't bring the white boys along." Alcorn

shook his head. "I swear, you cats don't make the least bit of sense. You really are out of your skulls."

"It's all right for you to talk," said Tip Harper. "You got it made."

"I got it made. Uh-huh, I sure have."

"You know how it was," said cousin Charlie. "How we had to fight up from Harlem."

"Didn't we, though?" Alcorn's voice became low and hard. "The playgrounds, huh, Charlie? Sneakers with holes in them, our feet burning on the asphalt. Summer and winter, indoors and out, fighting to learn the game."

"That's where the great ones come from. Back home," Charlie said. "Hillbillies and amateurs won't cut it."

"That's where we came from," said Alcorn. "Oh, I know. I remember well. I also remember something else. What about those that fell out?"

"Well . . . sure. That's the way it is."

"Those that dipped their beaks up in Harlem. Or they got to junkin' it. You mind Hiboy and Loboy? Best floor men ever walked? You mind them?"

"There's always some who fall out. What's that got to do with everything or anything?"

Alcorn said, "Rats in the tenements. Papa gone, mama working. Hungry and cold, hungry and hot. We always ran to the courts, you and me. One on one. Two on two. One on two. One on three. That was it, that was the way up. Make it in school, get to college. Give up everything to make it. You and me, Charlie, right?"

"We did it."

"By the grace of God, Charlie." Alcorn's voice deepened even further. "By the grace of the good Lord."

Someone snickered in the dark.

Alcorn turned his face toward the offender. "Laugh, you fool. That's the way it was with Loboy and Hiboy. They laughed. My mama and Charlie's mama are sisters. They saw to it we went to the meetin's. We didn't always have a real church. But an empty store, anyplace would do. We had meetin's and we sang. And we believed. And I believe now."

"You believe in whitey?"

"I believe in man. I don't believe in you coming here,

all soul brothers, all black, and trying to get me to go up against a good man, Hobie Reed. I don't believe in puttin' down players that haven't had a chance. That's what I don't believe in."

"Now wait, Bud. We want to make the playoffs. We don't get the money you get. We got wives and children. We figure you're the man. You got to have more say . . ."

Alcorn cut in. "I don't want more say! I am thirty-four years of age. It's not as easy to go out there and play as it used to be. It's not so easy to listen to the boos when things go wrong. And it's not as easy to listen to cats like you, either. Now do you want a beer or do you want to take your butts out of here and let me look at the stars?"

Charlie said, "Now coz, don't get uptight."

"I'm plenty uptight," Alcorn told him. "You want to call a team meeting, fine. But get the damn team here. Don't segregate us. There's plenty more blacks in the league than there is whites. Seems to me they got more of a right than you have."

"You are turning against your own kind," said Sam Felton. "I never believed you'd do that to us."

"Man, you are a dummy," said Alcorn. "I was in Alabama, I was with Dr. King. Where were you, Felton?"

"Well, I was in Harlem. How could I get down there?"

"You didn't half try," Alcorn said. "Look, I decided you can't have any of my draft beer from the keg. Just run along. Cousin'll show you the way out if you don't know it. I'll see you at practice tomorrow."

They went. They dared not bandy further words with him. He sat back. The stars were bright for a change, the smog had been light over the basin for a couple of days. After a while he began to talk in a murmur, a habit which had grown upon him lately in his loneliness.

"A star. High above in the sky. How is it up there, stars? It's not so good here. How long, oh Lord, how long?"

They had expected it of him since he had grown to seven feet and more in height. They had expected it at home, in school, in the pros. The people expected him to take charge. The sportswriters expected him to be superman always and forever. All the coaches before Hobie

Reed had demanded from him more than any man can give.

Hobie Reed understood basketball was a team game. Therein lay Bud Alcorn's hope.

"I was hard on them," he continued. "They come to me and they want and I can't give what they want. So I was hard on them. Good men, they're all good men. Sometimes they're like little children but they are good. Why do I have to play hard papa? Just a bit more taller'n cousin Charlie and I've got to be the Big Man. Nobody talks *with* me. People talk *at* me. Don't anyone know what it means to be alone?"

He had never married because the right woman had not come along. Either they had been impressed with his standing as an athlete or they had eyes on his money. His strong religious feeling kept him from making a fool of himself over them. The truth was he had never been in love, he admitted to himself.

He had read somewhere that it was always lonely at the top. Well, he wasn't the best player in the world; nobody was except on certain occasions. He was one of the best. The top was where he happened to live because he had grown so tall, he thought. That was his mountain peak, separating him from other men. He was just too damned big. People expected too much from big men.

Someday maybe he would get to coach a basketball team. He hoped so. He had a lot of ideas. He had known a lot of different kinds of people in his long career. It would be wonderful to work with them. It would be better, once removed from the burden of superstardom, to talk *with* them.

He got up and went into the house. He took down his special eighteen-ounce drinking goblet. He drew a draft beer from his built-in refrigerator that also dispensed icewater and soft drinks. He padded into his bedroom and turned on his hi-fi and a light and picked up the Bible.

Hobie Reed sat with Dorothy, his wife, in the den of their rented house in Canyon City's best neighborhood. They were staring at the television set but each was wrapped in private thoughts. The boys, Peter and Frank, ten and eleven, were in bed.

Dorothy was younger than her husband. She was a pretty woman with strength in her steady blue eyes and strong jawline. She knew the hard life, the constant moving, and the hiring and firing that went on in the world of professional sports.

She said, "You made the decision, Hobie. You've got to stick by it. Maybe he'll come around."

"Maybe," said Hobie Reed. "If we ever find him. He left in plenty of time to get here yesterday."

"You knew he was a crazy kid."

"I knew it, all right. But with the season coming on so soon I didn't think he was flakey enough not to show up."

"Are you going to fine him?"

"I have to. I have to think of the other players. I have to think of the kid I hired for less money than he's worth who's been working his tail off, the Brand boy."

"Will he be a help?"

"If trying counts he'll be a star." Hobie turned off the television set. "I don't know, darling. I just don't know. It was fish or cut bait. There was no way to go on with Kane. The bench just hasn't got the strength to go all the way. Everybody was leaning all the way on Bud. It's too late to make any kind of makeshift trade. I had to gamble."

"Is there any other way?" She smiled at him. "You've always taken your shots, Hobie. Sometimes they hit the mark. Sometimes they don't. It's our life."

"It's unfair. I know it. Moving the kids around from school to school, never owning our own house, always expecting to be fired . . ."

She said, "Hobie, we have stocks and bonds and we own property that pays rent. We have more than most people. The boys are happy. I'm happy."

He touched her hand. "You're a great girl."

"Tell me your plans." She knew he could get relief by talking with her, that he was afraid of boring her. She wanted to know. She could coach a basketball team herself just from the knowledge she had gained over the years of their marriage.

"It depends on the kids," he confessed. "I can start Peanuts at guard. If I can get five minutes out of him and then send in Jordan . . . if Jordan is that good, I'll have something."

"What about the Brand boy?"

"Same thing. I can use him in spots. If he learns enough he'll alternate with Jordan. Peanuts can then be used only in emergencies."

"You feel you're set at forward?"

"Krash is tough. Charlie Mount is good for a tall man. Maybe one of the kids could play the front court. That's the trouble. If we had a whole training season—but we haven't."

"And Bud has to go just about all the way."

"Just about. Farrell's another journeyman. But bless Bud's heart. He *wants* to play every minute."

"And he's the oldest man on the team."

"There's only one Bud Alcorn. There are other players, other superstars. But only one Bud."

"It's the same old gamble, then. We know about it."

"Kane is still a great competitor. I could have made a big mistake trading him off."

"Again, darling, it's the chance you take."

He said, "Without a wife and mother like you I'd be running scared all the time. I can hold the stone face to the world but you know how it is. Every coach has reason to suffer from ulcers."

"Not you, dear. We're against it."

"I leave my troubles on your doorstep."

She sang, "To the sunny side of the street. . . ."

They laughed. It was wonderful that they could laugh freely in the face of the complex problems which assailed them. They recognized and were grateful that they shared understanding.

The mother's ears, always attuned to the wavelength of her offspring, picked up the sound of voices from above. Hobie Reed followed her up the stairs to the room shared by the two boys.

There were double-tiered bunk beds. Frank had climbed

down from the upper and was standing beside young Peter. They were grinning when their parents flicked on the wall switch to light up the room.

Frank said, "He had a dream."

"Not a bad dream?"

"No," piped Peter, shaking his tousled head. "It was a beauty of a dream."

"About the Beavers," Frank said.

"It was real . . . real," said Peter. "I could see 'em. Playin'. I could see Bud and Charlie and Johnny and Red just as plain."

Hobie Reed hunkered down so that his head was on a level with those of his tow-headed sons. They were tall for their age and often mistaken for twins. Their blue eyes were only slightly clouded with sleep, their faces animated.

"He woke me up yellin' for the Beavers," said Frank. "Then he tumbled right out of bed."

"That's what you get for sleeping with basketballs instead of teddy bears like normal kids," said Hobie. "You dream of the game."

"It was a good dream," Peter insisted.

"Were we winning?"

"I don't know, really. But it was good."

"If we weren't winning how to you know it was good?" asked Hobie.

"Because."

"Because what?"

Frank burst forth, "Because he saw us in the playoffs!"

Hobie smiled at them. "I see. We were in the playoffs."

"I know it. I know we're goin' to make it," said Peter.

"Okay. You saw Bud and Charlie and Johnny and Red. So tell me, who was the fifth man?"

Peter slowly shook his head. "I didn't see him."

"Now that's a big help."

"I know. But he was there . . . like a blur. I don't know if it was Peanuts or one of the new fellas."

"Okay. You saw us in the playoffs. That's good enough. Now how about going back to sleep?"

"Oh, sure," said Peter. "That won't be any trouble." He climbed up into his berth.

Frank, the elder by a year, was staring at his father. "You think we got a chance?"

"Well, we're not in the hottest division," said Hobie cautiously. "We might luck in."

"I hope so. I really hope so."

"We all hope."

"Me and Peter, we like the school. They got a basketball program. Not many grade schools have basketball programs."

"I know." It was an ever-present worry, school for the boys.

"The kids are okay, too. Even the teachers."

"That's fine, Frank. We're glad you like the school."

"Even the principal," Frank said as a clinching argument. "He's a real keen Beaver fan."

"Right," said Hobie. "Now you get your sleep too, will you?"

"Oh, sure. Just wanted to remind you about the school."

Dorothy turned out the lights. They went into their bedroom.

Hobie said, "They know so much. They know if we make the playoffs my job is safe for a year or two."

"It's their life as much as it is ours," she replied.

"We may as well face it. The season depends on two kids. One's a green hand. The other's a flake."

"Are you going to sit up all night and worry about kids?" She laughed without strain. "Like you say, we hope a lot and pray a little—and you do your best."

"Yes," he said. "You're right as always."

But he lay awake wishing Peter had been able to distinguish the fifth man on the court. He had the superstitions of most people in athletics. The dream might just possibly be an omen. Of course nobody really believed in such signs. But—on the other hand—if he had an inkling as to who would be the key man in the playoffs, that is, if they got to the playoffs. . . .

He castigated himself for being a fool and resolutely closed his eyes.

4

The big auditorium echoed to the tune of bouncing basketballs and thudding rubber-soled shoes. The Beavers were practicing on their home court prior to the opening game of the season next week. Their exhibition games had been played and they were trying to form a combination minus their former star, Killer Kane.

Under one basket all but three of the squad were working on the basket, sharpening their eyes, passing the ball swiftly to one another, catching the unwary with hard tosses behind his back. At the other end Don Brand suffered the outrages and physical pain of enduring a two-on-one workout.

It was Red Farber, the topflight guard, and Peanuts Hopwood, the canny veteran, against the rookie. They did everything but steal his pants. They tooled him this way and turned the direction the other way. They shot over, under, and around him, scoring repeatedly. They blocked his every endeavor after he took the rebound from the board. They had him hot and cold and embarrassed in turn.

Don was highly conscious of the watchful eyes of Coach Hobie Reed during this entire torture period. He could not estimate in his mind how well—or how poorly—he was doing. He could only doggedly keep trying. It was like a schoolyard boy's trick when they stole a book from a kid and kept passing it around just beyond his frantic reaching. Of course the experienced schoolboy would soon weary of his pursuit and would shrug and quit, knowing his tormentors would then lose interest. Not so with the Beaver forwards; they seemed to enjoy the unequal contest.

Don thought he would collapse. His condition was good but nobody, he thought, panting, could keep this up for long. At that moment the coach's whistle blew, demanding attention from all. Don collapsed on the bench with a towel into which he dipped his flaming face.

When he looked up he saw directly opposite from him the lounging figure of Oscar "Beans" Jordan. There were telltale circles beneath the eyes of the new man, and he was still wearing the mod clothing, now a bit soiled and rumpled, in which he had set forth for Las Vegas, Nevada. He also wore a small defiant grin.

He said, "Well, folks, here I am—your savior. How much is my side trip goin' to cost me?"

"Five hundred dollars," said Coach Reed without expression.

"Worth it," nodded Jordan. He smiled at them all. "Reckon we all know each other. Right?"

Reed said, "There's an equipment man in the locker room. He'll fit you for a suit."

Jordan raised a limp hand. "Man, I been whoopin' it up. Needed a change, like, y' know? I need a sleep."

"Suit up or it'll cost you another five hundred." Reed did not raise his voice. The Beavers stood staring without speaking, stony-faced. Don could feel the enmity for the newcomer burgeoning like a dark cloud.

Jordan winced. "Now, that's too much. No way I can afford that. Las Vegas wasn't real good to me, y' know? Just about did break even on the crap tables."

"Play or pay," said Reed.

It was a moment that would make or break, Don thought. Jordan could really blow it—which meant that Reed's job would be in dire jeopardy—or he could do the right thing.

The new man lifted a shoulder. "Boss man may not be right alla time—but he's the boss man."

He lifted a languid hand and strolled toward the locker room. Don heaved a sigh of relief.

Coach Reed said, "Bud, I'd like a half-speed workout of the squad. You know what we need."

"Right, coach," said Alcorn.

With no further fuss the starters, including Peanuts

Hopwood, took their places. The reserves obediently took their places in opposition. Don sat alongside the coach on the bench.

Reed said, "You catch onto my system very well."

"I believe in it," Don said. "Teamwork, keep moving with or without the ball, pass to the open man."

"And stress the fundamentals," added Reed. "You're doing well. I knew you had the fundamentals. It's a question of adjusting to the professional style."

"Thanks," said Don dryly. "I think I'm half-dead but thanks anyway."

"It'll take time," Reed warned. "Never believe it won't."

"I'm convinced."

"Watch the way Johnny Krash sets it up," said Reed, directing attention to the court. "Bud goes down on the low post as quickly as he can. Farber brings the ball down. Johnny is moving, taking the sideline while Peanuts follows. If they take that sideline away from us we go to Charlie, or back to Farber after he passes off and sets himself. If they double-team us, we don't go crosscourt. Never go crosscourt. Try and keep it where they can't intercept no matter what else happens."

Don listened. Reed went on in his patient way, firm, decisive, but without domination of his audience. It was all gospel, information Don had half-known, half-imagined, so that he nodded, following the discourse. It was the real pro game and he soaked it up like a sponge.

He watched the men on the floor, superb athletes going through the motions in half-time. They all had been the best. Alcorn was like no other man who had ever played the game, a giant in every sense of the word. But Bud was thirty-four and wore elastic supports on both knees. Every other veteran had his history of injuries. For a certain time they were superb, unbeatable. Then they needed a rest. It was up to the reserves and Don knew it was up to him and to Beans Jordan rather more than the others.

Now Beans Jordan appeared. His shorts appeared very brief. His stockings were high to his knees. Nothing about him was orthodox including the Indian headband which bound up his blond crop of hair.

Reed still did not raise his voice. "Jordan, go in for Hopwood please."

Beans blinked. "For Hopwood?"

"It's necessary that you learn. Since you're late you can learn best by going into the action."

"Well . . . okay."

Peanuts, weary from the earlier workout, was glad to come out, Don knew. They sat together beside the coach. They watched Beans Jordan take the court.

"They'll kill him," said Peanuts.

"If I'd started him with the reserves they'd have really murdered him," Reed agreed. "We have to learn about him quick, right now."

Peanuts, always a happy character, said, "If we can shake him loose often enough he'll gun for us."

"But everyone knows that," replied Reed. "We have to look for him to be double-teamed."

"Right," said Peanuts. He grinned at Don. "That's where you come in. They don't know about you. Not yet."

"If I get into a game at all I'll feel lucky," said Don. "I knew it'd be different but wow! It's another world."

"You do good, man," said Peanuts. "Don't he do good, coach?"

"He does better than I hoped," said Reed.

They were silent watching the movement on the court. When Jordan entered the game Bud had given the signal to speed it up. It was not slow motion any longer. The first-string players were moving the ball, trying to get it to the new guard.

Beans took a pass. He was immediately challenged by George Farrell, who was six feet seven inches and, although not a topflight player, had the muscles of a sideshow strong man. As Jordan tried to go around Farrell, in came Ed Carey.

Jordan dribbled behind his back in a flashy maneuver to throw off Carey. Farrell leaned into him. The ball bounced away. Carey grabbed it. Jordan had committed a turnover the first time he got his hands on the ball—a cardinal sin in the pro grame.

Peanuts said, "He spends a year in the league and don't forget the kid stuff. Crazy, man."

Reed did not speak. It was not his procedure to criticize a player either publicly or to teammates. He preferred to give his lectures in private. But his face was stony.

Don kept his eyes on the action. Undaunted, the flop-haired Jordan was pursuing Carey. When the reserve guard shot for the basket and missed Jordan leaped high in the air. He almost got hold of the ball. Then Farrell once more leaned into him, dropping an elbow on his shoulder.

Jordan did not get the rebound. He shook his head, grinning as Carey again tried and this time made the two points.

Red Farber again took the ball down for the regulars. Jordan moved a little faster now, free-lancing, unsure of the direction of the Beaver flow to the basket. Farrell blocked his path. He faked and went outside. Farber gave him a sharp pass. He was thirty feet from the basket.

Jordan set, aimed, and lofted a shot. It went high above outstretched arms. It fell swishing through the hoop.

Jordan said loudly, "That's what I'm here for, you cats."

"A real gunner," said Peanuts without enthusiasm. "He didn't have any right to take that one, much less make it."

"He's in there cold," the coach said. "Don, you take him out. I want to talk with him. I've seen enough."

"Good shooter, no defense," said Peanuts out of his long experience as Don went onto the floor and sent Jordan to the bench.

Joining the regulars, Don wondered. The way Jordan had tossed in the long shot, without apparent strain, his utter confidence that it would go into the basket, was most impressive. The attitude of the gunner was another matter.

Bud Alcorn was saying, "We slow down again. Brand, you're beginning to get with it. Watch the moves, get open, keep on the jump all the time. We play defense and we play offense also, you dig?"

"I'm trying to dig," said Don.

"Yeah, man," said Alcorn. "You try." He cast a short look at the bench where Reed was talking earnestly and without heat to the new man.

Charlie Mount said, "It was a bad deal. That hillbilly will cause nothing but trouble."

"Cousin, you're bad-mouthin' again," Alcorn warned him. "Just play the game the way Reed wants."

The workout continued. Under the slowdown procedure there was no attempted stealing of the ball as the men went through patterns which they would use in a game. They would use them subconsciously, Don had learned. There were not set plays except in tight situations with the clock running out. It was a matter of learning your teammates, learning their style, trying to get one man open at the key spot and the right time for an easy shot. Failing that, there were moves designed to open a hole through which a shooter could drive to the basket. It was all a problem of superb athletes going at top speed and trying their skills against men as strong and sharp as themselves. It was like putting a machine together, and Don Brand had to fit himself into the mechanical whole as an important cog.

Alcorn and Krash were the superstars, he had found. They almost never committed a mental error. Farber was in their class, a marvelous floor man. Mount was next in quality. For a few moments Peanuts Hopwood was as good as anybody. After them Don felt that he had a chance to beat out anyone for the sixth place on the team.

Anyone except Jordan, he thought. If the former All American could fit in any place with his remarkable shooting eye he would be most valuable. Again it was the total machine that counted. Individual skill had to be controlled under Coach Reed's system of unselfish team play.

Reed finally blew his whistle. The day's work was concluded. Don walked toward the showers alongside the towering Alcorn. It seemed strange to him still that he had to crane up to look at Alcorn—he was himself six feet three.

The center and captain spoke quietly. "You've got the attitude, Don. I like that."

It was the first time Alcorn had addressed him by his given name and Don felt a grateful glow. "Coach Reed makes it clear. There's a beat to the play. A rhythm, I guess you'd call it."

"All us black men got rhythm."

Don protested, "Hey, now, wait. I didn't mean . . ."

"I know what you meant," said Alcorn. "Some of the others, well, they don't listen to what you mean. They listen to what you say."

"That's a warning, isn't it?"

"Not exactly. A friendly tip, maybe. I'm afraid there's going to be a problem with our hillbilly friend."

"I thought he showed some class. He didn't get uptight when they leaned on him."

"Class? Or plain ego?"

"Well, he took it with a smile."

"Like he's too big to worry. I've known some actors and actresses since I've been out here," said Alcorn. "It's like they're children playing big lady or big man. On this club there's no room for any more supermen." He laughed. "And that's a horse on me."

They dressed. They came back out into the auditorium. Don was almost to the exit when Kitty McCoy appeared from the shadows. He stopped, astounded.

"Hello, stranger," she said.

"How did you get in here?"

"There are ways and means. Good workout, was it?"

"Good enough." He was puzzled. "I haven't seen you in a week."

"Nor your father since you moved out of his house," she said. "He wonders a little."

"But I've been busy morning, noon and night," he protested. "I'm a raw rookie, I've had to spend every hour studying fundamentals, movies of last year's games—a million details."

"Your father's still your father."

"Did he send you here?"

"Let's say he gave me a hint—and a way to get in. He owns part of the company that holds the mortgage on the building. Or did you know?"

"You know a lot more than I about his business. Tell me, how is my buddy Homer?"

"He's fine. He takes a lady to dinner and treats her kindly."

"Good Lord, Kitty, are you going to be like that? You've got a real nerve. You date Homer and then you come down on me for not calling or something."

"Are we quarreling?" she asked too brightly. "I could comment on your date, the little Martha."

He had to laugh. "Hey, we're acting like we were back in Westwood in high school. Come on, Kitty, you know you're number one with me. Always have been."

"That's nice." She squeezed his hand. "I've missed you."

"I'm glad. Can you come and dine with me now?"

"I planned on it."

"Good. How about the Tail o' the Cock in the Valley? A nice drive there and back."

"Suits me," she said.

They left her car in the parking lot and took the convertible and drove eastward and into the San Fernando Valley traffic. They ate in the fine old restaurant and then drove back to Canyon City on the freeway, taking the slow lane, talking as they had in the past. When they came again to her parked car they sat a moment. It was a pleasant moonlit night in southern California.

She said, "You can't expect your father to really understand, you know."

"He understands. He just won't believe. I'm into a whole new thing. Try to make him see that."

"You're changing. I can see it."

"Am I? Is that why you haven't called me 'Junior' tonight?"

"Maybe." She paused, then said, "Homer asked me to marry him."

It was a shock, yet he was not surprised, not really. He said, "No way."

"Why not?"

"He has no humor."

"He has his own brand."

"You trying to tell me it's your kind of humor?"

"People have to adjust."

"Why should you think of marriage now? You've got a good job. You like it at the company. You're young."

"All women think of marriage. At least my kind do."

"Is that so?" He was genuinely amazed. "I thought you new women were self-sufficient."

"You think a lot of things." She got out of the car before he could prevent her. "Call your father."

"Oh, sure, as soon as I get home," he assured her. Then he called, "Hey!"

"Yes?"

"Go marry Homer and never laugh again."

She turned on her heel, got into her car and drove off. He sat thinking about her. It was too heavy for him, he told himself, too heavy. He started the convertible and drove to his new apartment near the auditorium where the Beavers played. It was a four-room-and-bath place, furnished coldly and efficiently with a large refrigerator and a king-sized bed, the latter two items a real pleasure for him. He dialed his home.

His father said, "Hello? Brand speaking."

"Hello, father."

"Well . . . how are you, Junior?"

"Working like a pair of dogs."

"That hard? I thought it was—more like a game. Fun."

"It's more like digging ditches. But it is fun all right."

"You enjoy the hard work?"

"You bet. Hey, I saw Kitty. Sorry I haven't called but it's been busy time."

"Busy time? I see . . . You sound like a different man."

"Maybe I do. Maybe I am different."

There was a small silence. His father said, "Don't overdo it, Junior. You have a heritage whether you like it or not. Don't become—what is it? A jockstrap?"

Don laughed freely. "Father? I already am a jock. Don't worry about it, will you? A fella can only play basketball till he's in his thirties. It's not a lifetime job."

"Then what happens?"

"Maybe I get to coach. Maybe even like you said, coach a company squad. Athletics are healthy, you know. Sound minds in sound bodies?"

"You joke, of course. Well, I wish you luck."

"Thanks, father. Talk to you soon."

"Good night, Junior."

"Good night, father."

He shook his head and went to his beloved refrigerator. Since working out with the Beavers he had been constantly hungry and thirsty. He had always thought himself a strong, rugged big man but he had learned he needed more weight, more muscle. He found yogurt, beef extract, honey and milk. He put them all into a blender, added a dollop of brandy and switched on the motor. As an afterthought he cut up a slightly soft banana and put it in with the rest of the rather disgusting mess. Then he got out a huge tumbler, cracked ice, picked up a new book, *Basketball—Offense and Defense*, by Hobie Reed and retired to his bedroom.

Not far away Beans Jordan parked the Maserati at the swinging-singles apartment he had come to like a homing pigeon. He was dead-tired from his all-night session in Las Vegas plus the workout and long lecture he had received after joining the Beavers. He glanced toward the big swimming pool as he headed for his ground-floor habitation. He stopped dead.

The soft light shone upon a blonde girl in a swimsuit. She poised, then dove into the water.

Beans rushed into his apartment on the double. He stripped off his clothing and donned a pair of baggy modern shorts. He skipped out again and sat by the side of the pool and waited and watched.

The girl climbed out of the water. Her hair was long and untrammeled by a disfiguring cap. She was breathtakingly beautiful. She walked toward a nearby chair where her towel was folded.

"How's the water?" asked Beans brightly, giving her his best grin.

"Try it and find out," she said without interest. Then she did a double take. "Oh. You're Beans Jordan."

"Himself in person." He was on his feet extending his hand.

"I've read about you." She barely touched his fingers. She began wiping herself with the towel.

"Don't believe all that crap," he told her. "I'm just a lonely old boy from the hills."

"A lonely old swinger," she said.

"Anything wrong with that?" He was examining her

closer. He said, "Hey, I've seen you somewhere. No joke. I mean, it's no line, like. I really have."

She relented a trifle. "On the tube."

"Television! You're an actress."

"Well, not much of an actress. I'm the secretary in 'That Detective.'"

"Sure. They give you two lines but they show you in a bathing suit a lot. A bikini."

"That's why I wear this. I hate bikinis since I'm in that show."

Now they were launched in conversation. They sat down and looked at one another. They smiled.

She said, "I'm not a swinger. I'm not very bright, either. So I have to be careful."

"But you know me. Everybody don't know me now will get to know me."

"You've got the brass all right."

"Brass?"

"You know. You move in."

"Not always," he said piously. "I only like nice girls if you really want to know."

"But you don't go with nice girls."

"I seldom meet any." He made a sad face. "A man gets to be somebody you should see 'em, the kind that flock around."

"You think it's any different with a girl?"

"Worse, I expect." He was now all sympathy. "Tell me about your career."

She needed no further urging. She was a simple girl, at that, he thought. She came from the Midwest and she had won the local beauty contest and they sent her to Hollywood. She attended a drama school but everyone said she couldn't act and never would learn. Then a director had seen a photograph of her and recognized that she was a true camera pet—there was no angle from which she did not register beauty. So he had put her in some small parts.

"He wasn't a nice man," she said. "Now I work for an older director. He's real nice. They treat me like I'm a lady. The pay is all right. Enough. I'm getting a lot of what they call exposure."

"I'll say!" He coughed, covering up. "I mean, hey, how about you and me go out and see the town? I just got here. You could show me."

"You're supposed to be in training or something, aren't you?"

"I'm a pro," he told her. "Pros work all season. They have to relax. Everybody knows that."

"Oh," she said. "You're sure it's all right?"

"It's wonderful, baby," he told her. "Throw on any old thing. I'll be right with you."

He went to his apartment and donned his goin'-out clothing: a double-knit wide-lapeled suit, high collar open at the neck, a wraparound scarf, buckled boots. He put a wad of cash in his pocket. He ignored the circles beneath his eyes. He was whistling merrily when he went out to greet—what was her name?

He remembered from the television credits. "Alicia Aster." Playing Marie the secretary to the private eye in the series. A nothing part for a dumb broad . . . but she was nice . . . he could tell that she was nice . . . he had only been half-kidding about that. Life had been hectic. There had been a bunch of dames and none of them had been more than a night's fun. Since he was settled into Canyon City he might as well have one nice girl he could sort of date regular.

"Alicia Aster." It was a good enough name. She sure was as pretty as a little speckled hen . . . a BIG speckled hen. . . .

5

The Beavers opened the long season against the Banshees from the East in a two-game series at home. Don Brand was preparing to leave for the auditorium when his phone rang.

Martha Hall's voice said, "I'm so glad I got you. We all want to wish you luck."

"Aren't you going to the game?"

"Of course. Pa has season tickets for the family. But we thought we'd talk to you while you're alone."

"That's real swell," said Don. Again he felt the warmth of friendship coming from the Halls.

She said, "Hope we see you before you leave on the road trip."

"Hey, how about after the game? I won't be eating dinner before we play. Okay?"

"Not the Now Then," she said wryly.

"No. The Tail?"

"You're sure you want me?"

"You're my luck," said Don.

"All right, then. Here's Pa."

He talked to all the Halls. They teased him, told him he might get killed by the professional sharpsters—and hoped he would score thirty points. They were fine people, he thought, hanging up and going down to his car.

There were few cars in the parking lot at this early hour. But as he walked toward the players' entrance a couple came toward him waving a greeting. It was Kitty and Homer Sanders.

She said, "We wanted to wish you luck and all that."

"Yes," said Homer. "The best, Don."

"Thanks," said Don. "It's good of you."

"We thought we'd see you before we had dinner," said Homer. "Are you all right? Is everything as you expected?"

"More so," said Don.

"You put on a little weight, didn't you?" asked Kitty.

"Had to," he replied. "It's a rough league."

"Well . . . we're rooting for you."

"Is father coming to the game?"

"Oh, no. But he sent his regards."

"Uh-huh. Well, thanks again." He watched them go to Homer's black Cadillac. He should be jealous, he supposed. Kitty had sort of been his girl for a long time and Homer had asked her to marry him. It was odd, but he could not be jealous of Homer. The man just didn't fit the image of the successful suitor.

Beans Jordan's Maserati growled in and parked alongside Don's convertible. The blond youth came and looked after the departing couple.

"Hey, man. Who's the doll with the shape?"

"Hi, Beans. Oh, that's my father's secretary."

"Yeah? Your old man's got an eye for gams."

"Don't you believe it. Kitty's efficient. My father runs on those lines. He'd be a great coach."

"Speakin' of coaches. Reed's drivin' me up the wall, y' know? Man, talk about efficiency. He crabs about every move I make."

They went inside the building. Don said, "Coach sees all, knows all. Did you read his book?"

"Book? He wrote a book?" Jordan was truly surprised.

"You'd better get it and maybe you'll understand him better."

"Me? Read a *book?*" He shook his head. "Man, they bugged me with them books in college. It hurts my eyes to read. And you know I need my eyes real bad."

"Nobody has better vision," Don told him. "Look, I'm a raw rookie. You've had a year in the league. But—just between us—you ought to get with the coach. I mean, he's trying to make a real superstar out of you."

"You can't kill a dead dog," said Jordan cheerfully. "I already am a superstar. When Reed catches on he'll start me and everybody'll know it."

They had reached the dressing room. Only Bud Alcorn and Charlie Mount were on hand at this early hour. Jordan's last breezy statement hung in the air. He waved at the two big cousins and went toward the last locker at the end of the long row. "Hiya, big men? Here's your little helper."

Don's locker was near that of Mount. Alcorn sat with his legs stretched out, staring toward Jordan. Sometimes the big man brooded like a prophet of yore. Without looking up he spoke to Don.

"You know where that cat was last night? Jiggin' at the New Look with a gorgeous blonde lady. Closed the joint."

"He had all day to sleep."

"All day he and the gal were swimmin' and laughin' it up at that place where they live."

"How do you know all this?" asked Don curiously. "Have we got detectives following us?"

"Nothin' like it. We've got fans and friends. They call. Charlie—he's always nosy. I don't go along with him but sometimes it's interesting. Superstar is superswinger."

"Coach knew that when he traded for him, didn't he?"

"Uh-huh. Coach has tried to reason with him. Charlie and the boys are not happy with the result."

"They leaned on him. It didn't help."

"They were thinking about the freeze."

"You mean ignoring him? Not speaking to him?"

"That's their notion."

"I'm against it," said Don. "It'll only alienate him further."

Bud Alcorn said, "Y' know, rookie, you've got more sense than anybody exceptin' maybe me."

"Thanks."

"You know about the Banshees, right? Eight men running all night? Run and shoot? Wear us old folks down like they did last year?"

"That's what Hobie told me."

"You and that flake. You could run with them."

"Maybe."

"You could. Both of you."

"If you say so, captain." Don grinned. "You and Hobie are boss men."

"Farrell will spell me some tonight and tomorrow. Peanuts will go a fast five. Then you. The flake, there, he'll go in for spots. Krash and Farber, they've got to go as far as they can, then a little bit more. You see how that puts it on you kids right at the start?"

"I see."

"And Beans-boy is out all night and having fun all afternoon with his girl friend."

"He believes in fun."

"So do I. But fun is several different things. Be ready to work this weekend, rookie."

"I guess I see what you mean."

He dressed. Charlie Mount drew Bud aside and talked to him, angry, gesticulating. Don had begun to suspect that Mount was a trouble seeker and that several of his friends agreed with him. Only the blunt, sardonic Alcorn kept the lid on what could be a boiling pot of dissent— and the season had not yet even begun.

Mount came to his locker mumbling, paying no attention to Don's greeting. Coach Reed and the rest of the players appeared. Don finished dressing and waited for the pregame talk.

It was brief. "You'll have eight men running all the time," said Reed. "Gale, Smith, Byron, Field, Cohen and the three from the bench, Hobson, Grant and Hagen. And a little guy named Dowell who can shoot if you don't cover him tight. Any questions?"

There were none. They went out in sweat suits and warmed up. They came back and rested a moment. The auditorium was filling up well for the first game.

Reed said, "You're pros, you know the importance of drawing in the people. A good start will make new fans in this new town. A bad start may leave us in the cold. This is as important as any game we'll play this season. Let's go."

They went out and shot a few baskets. The Banshees, Don thought, were not impressive in size but they moved like oiled robots on wheels. Their coach, Markson, preferred greyhounds to muscle men.

The Hall family were close to the Beaver bench, a cheering squad in themselves. The management had hired pompom girls from a nearby college and the crowd was noisy and good-natured for a start. They had to be shown, of course. Hobie Reed was entirely correct. They applauded each Beaver as he was introduced with a special loud yell for Don, the hometown man.

Then the starters took the court, with Peanuts Hopwood in the guard position. Don sat on the bench next to Beans Jordan.

Beans said, not caring who heard, "I should be in there instead of Peanuts. I'll show them runts."

"Just shut up and watch, will you?" Don said. "You'll be in there soon enough."

"Right on," said the irrepressible Jordan. His use of slightly dated jive with his hillbilly accent was amusing but he could be annoying at a time like this. Don was as taut as a drumhead on a dry day.

It seemed an hour before the striped shirt at center court raised a hand, then put the ball into the air. Bud Alcorn leaped high over Byron of the Banshees and tipped back to Red Farber, who took the ball and described a sharp circle as he came down toward the Beaver basket. Peanuts crossed over. The Banshees moved like a set of five wheels but Peanuts had the ball and was giving it back to Farber who had followed through.

Red faked for the basket and passed behind his back. Bud took the ball on the high post and revolved like a giant statue in ebony, finger-rolling the ball. It went through for two.

Field put the ball into play for the Banshees. Now the speed of the visitors was plain to see. They flew around the boards. Peanuts Hopwood went with them. For the few minutes he could last the Beaver guard was as swift as a swallow in flight.

The Banshees came down. They tried for a corner setup. Peanuts was all over Gale, the forward. Krash shifted to help. Gale tried a bounce pass. Farber, foreseeing the play, was in the way.

Alcorn had been slow getting down with the fast-breaking Banshees. Farber took the ball and heaved it high. Bud reached for it, saw Peanuts springing, led with a low, swift throw. As if it were all planned far in advance,

Peanuts took the pass and went in for an easy layup. Beavers four, Banshees zero, and Jordan laughed on the bench.

"That's real neat, man," he said. "Neat. Now watch."

Again the Banshees came out from under the basket. This time the speed had increased. They were incredibly quick getting the ball into play. They assumed the right sideline and something had to give. Peanuts kept up with them but he was alone. They got the ball to their shooter, Smith. He wheeled and dealt to the hoop.

Up into the air went Charlie Mount. He spatted the ball with his big hand and forced it back down at Smith. It bounced off the amazed Banshee forward's shoulder. Peanuts was on it like a squirrel gathering nuts in May.

Krash and Farber were sprinting. Don had forgotten how fast the Beavers could be when they were fresh and the adrenaline was flowing. The ball went to Bud, then to Mount, who jumped, seemed to hang, then shot. The basket was good for two and it became Beavers six, Banshees zero, and the home crowd came alive and shook the rafters with loud noises.

Jordan drawled, "How long you reckon we can keep it up?"

Nobody replied. Everyone but Beans was on the edge of the bench exhorting their teammates to go, go, go. They were professionals but they had their enthusiasms, mainly for perfection on the court. The Beavers were playing perfect basketball.

The Banshees did not show the least emotion or excitement. They did not bother with a time out to talk it over. They just continued to relentlessly take the ball down as fast as possible—and considerably faster than most teams. They were really not deceptive, not tricky. They merely moved the ball and took their shots. They got past Peanuts for once.

Farber came in but the ball went to Smith. This time Mount went up too quickly as Smith faked him. The Banshee deadeye flipped the ball through the net. Beavers 6, Banshees 2.

In a moment it was 6 to 4. Then there were three fouls in a row. Result, Beavers 7, Banshees 6.

Now they began guarding so close that neither team could score. The ball went up, bounded into the hands of the man nearest, then went downcourt, then another try, then back up the boards again. Peanuts was flagging as five minutes of the first half ticked by.

Reed signaled and Alcorn asked for time out. The subs arose and the starters sat down and mopped. Reed stood before them.

The coach said, "Peanuts, take a rest. Jordan, you try it and see if you can match their speed."

"I can beat it," said Beans stripping off his jacket.

"Look for the open man," Reed told him for the hundredth time. "If you take a long shot against these birds they'll block it or they'll steal it and stuff it down your throat."

"I've played them before," Beans said. It was never certain whether he ever heard advice or criticism. He seemed to dwell in a cheerful world of his own where he was king.

The team went back on the court. Reed beckoned to Don to sit beside him.

"If he'd play up and then get loose and shoot over them a few times he could scare them," Reed said. "If they change their style we can beat them. When you go in will you remember that?"

"Yes, sir," said Don. He glued his eyes to the play action.

Jordan always moved the same way, as if he were loafing. But he accepted a pass from Krash in-bounds and ran clean away from Field, the guard assigned to him. He dribbled down to the post and gave the ball to Alcorn, then went in.

Alcorn handed off to Krash who was immediately covered. Jordan broke for the corner and Krash led him. Jordan took the ball, whirled and shot without looking. It was a clean two points. Jordan raised a clenched fist and yelled, "Here we go! Beans is on tonight!"

The crowd loved it but it was an ordinary shot, Don knew. The scoreboard changed to Beavers nine, Banshees six. The Banshees were running again. They were absolutely tireless, it seemed. They had not yet inserted their other three swifties.

They scored. It became a one-point ball game again. The Beavers attacked. The Banshees were all over them. The ball went to Jordan. Thirty feet out he shot for the hoop. He missed.

Coach Reed said, "Brand."

Don went into the game. Jordan laughed as he went to the bench.

There had been a man open—Farber—when Jordan had taken the long shot, Don knew. He wondered if Beans would have been removed had the ball gone into the basket—and decided that two points would not have altered Reed's action.

The score was still Beavers nine, Banshees eight. Bud Alcorn battled the opposition for the ball and got hold of it, sticking out his elbows, looking around. He found Farber and the Beavers made their move to open a lane.

It was Don Brand's first experience in a league game. He found it to be like swimming against a strong tide. No matter where he moved there was a tough, masterful resistance. It was as if the Banshees knew precisely what he must do and were to a man determined that he should not succeed.

Elbows caught him. Hands were laid legally upon him. Fingers illegally snatched at his trunks. Bodies were in his path. He was quick and strong but they were equal in every way. True to Reed's coaching he never stopped moving.

The Banshees moved with them but he was keeping a man busy. The ball went around and around as the superb defense prevented a shot until the twenty-four-second clock was running out. Then Charlie Mount had to try one over Cohen's head.

It missed. Don went for the rebound. He was shoved aside. The referee did not call the foul. Byron had the ball for the Banshees. Don ran down the court on defense as fast as he could go. He double-teamed Smith, the gunner, along with Farber. Smith managed to pass to Gale, and the other Banshee forward scored. They went ahead for the first time in the game, ten to nine.

Farber came downcourt with fire in his eye, bent low, dribbling around a Banshee defender. Don went to the right, where the play was being set up by Krash and the others. Alcorn took the post and a pass went to him high above his head. He was guarded closely by Byron. He saw Don circling and gave him the ball.

Don had one tiny instant of free time. He was standing just outside the circle. He went up and made his jump and tried for the hoop.

It went through. He had scored his first two-pointer. As he came down an elbow again struck his ribs. A receipt from the Banshees he thought, elated at having put the Beavers back in the lead at eleven to ten.

From then on he was in a dogfight. The Banshees scored. Krash scored. The Banshees scored. Alcorn scored. It went at a furious pace, feet pounding on the slick boards, men whirling and running and stopping and going.

Don scored again. The Banshees came right back with two. Fouls were exchanged. The Beavers each picked up one. The Banshees collected their share.

It was forty-five for the Beavers, forty-four for the Banshees with a few minutes of the half left and the crowd in turmoil at the close play of the professionals. The Banshees took a time out.

At the Beaver bench Coach Reed was watching the Banshees. Three fresh players were shucking their jackets. The opposition was about to utilize its solid bench.

Reed said, "Peanuts, Felton . . . Jordan. Go in and keep playing our game. Feed the free man. Make them cover you at all times. They'll run. Run with them!"

Don sat down with Farber and Mount. All were winded and sweating. But Alcorn and Krash were still out there, going the full distance. It was a terrific test of stamina.

Reed was saying, "Keep on top of them all the time. It's the only way to handle them. We're getting our share of the baskets. We're even on rebounds."

Mount muttered, "That Jordan boy can't defend against 'em. I'll bet anything he can't."

Play was resumed. Now the Banshees seemed swifter, if anything. The fresh men went pelting down the court and surrounded the basket. Jordan was in the melee but someone put a pick on him and the Banshees scored to go ahead again at forty-six to forty-five.

Peanuts brought the ball downcourt. The veteran was like a cricket, all elbows and knees and moving left, then right, zigzagging through the defenders. He found Bud on the post and went to the corner. Alcorn tried to pass back to him.

Hagen, the fresh Banshee guard, deserted Jordan, who was a moment late following him. The ball was deflected. Hobson had it for the Banshees and the flow reversed itself like a fast-receding tide. The Banshees went down and scored.

Again Peanuts whizzed downcourt. Alcorn went to the high post to take the pass and tried to wheel and score. Grant, the sub center for the Banshees, jumped a mile into the air and slapped away the ball. Again the Banshees went roaring toward their hoop. Again they scored. It was now fifty to forty-five for the visitors.

Charlie Mount said it aloud this time. "Jordan just can't cut it, that's all."

Now the clock was showing the last few seconds. The Banshees went man to man to prevent a final score by the Beavers. They swarmed all over Peanuts. He managed to get the ball to Farrell, who was promptly double-teamed.

At midcourt Jordan was all alone. He yelled sharply, "Here, George, here!"

Farrell desperately passed back to Jordan, who glanced at the clock, then flipped the ball into the air.

Turning over and over the basketball dropped gently into the net and nestled, then dropped free. It was an incredible shot—it could not be called sheer luck. It made the score Banshees fifty, Beavers forty-seven as the horn blew to end the half.

Jordan put a hand over his heart and bowed deeply to the cheering fans. Then he pranced off the floor waving two fingers for either peace or victory. Don was walking past the Hall family. They were mildly clapping but Pat Hall leaned over and spoke to Don.

"That's the way to win there, pal. That's the name of the game."

"Thanks," Don said, going on toward the dressing room.

Charlie Mount fumed, "The lucky showboat. Takin' bows after the way he played."

"He did sink it," Don answered. "He's got the guts of a bear."

"And the hungry belly," said Mount. The other players within hearing nodded agreement.

In the locker room there was silence. Bruises and scrapes were attended to by the trainer. Coach Reed leaned against the wall next to the blackboard waiting for the squad to simmer down. Don washed his wrists and face and soaked his head. Jordan was singing a hillbilly tune to himself, still grinning in self-appreciation.

They might not like him, Don thought, but Beans had scored the two points to narrow the gap before intermission, a morale builder every time. Whatever they thought, it made a terrific difference to have an accurate long shooter on the squad. Coach Reed had to know it. The coach's problem was how to handle it and Don was glad it was not his personal problem.

Coach Reed spoke. "Bud . . . what do you think?"

Alcorn replied, "I think I'm glad they're not in our division. They about run a man to death."

"But they're only as strong as their bench."

"Right," said Alcorn. He looked around. "I can go all the way. I wouldn't ask it of anybody else."

"I can do it," said Krash.

"Yes," agreed the coach. "Now it's going to be up to the rest of you."

Jordan piped up, "Just let me shoot. I'll bring them out and bust 'em up."

"No," said Reed coolly, dispassionately. "That's not our game. It's not the right game. Not for any team. Too risky. You made one good shot, Jordan. You missed one. The percentage is bad."

"You're the boss man," said Jordan, smiling on blissfully.

Reed said, "No use to talk. Save your breath for running. As Bud says, they keep coming. Meet them and beat them."

Don had heard stories of pro coaches who ranted and raved at their teams. Reed was low key, all right. He dealt with the players as though they were responsible adults. The question remained: were they all?

They went out for the second half. The regulars started with Don on the bench alongside Jordan.

The gunner said, "I just take my pay check and do what the boss man says. But the way I do it—I knock 'em off their feet with the goodies. Then you can eat 'em up."

"Uh-huh," said Don. There was something likable about the wrong-headed blond youth. He was aggravating and he might cause plenty of trouble for the team but Don couldn't dislike him.

The play began. The flow of the game did not alter. It was breathtaking, swift basketball at its best. The score mounted without altering. The Banshees clung to their lead of three points. The coaches substituted, players came and went, still there was that difference on the electric scoreboard.

Don thought he was learning in his allotted playing time. Once he switched off and double-teamed Smith, their shooter, and stole the ball. He passed it far downcourt to Alcorn, who went in for a layup. The Hall family led the riotous cheers. But the Banshees remained three points in the lead and the clock began, as always, to run its course.

Reed called a time out. Alcorn dropped onto the bench, dog-tired. Jordan and Don Brand had not been in the game for the last few minutes.

Reed said, "I'm going to try something. Bud—you're beat. You need a few moments. I'm putting in Farrell and Brand and Jordan. We want three points."

"Four points," cried Jordan. "I want four."

"Get us three and Bud goes back in with Peanuts and Red."

Alcorn said, "I don't know, coach. I don't know . . ."

"It's a gamble," said Reed. "We have to gamble."

Time was called. Don had not been on the court with Jordan before now. He missed the reliable Farber. He missed the giant presence of Alcorn. As Farber's replacement, and because of Jordan's flakiness, it was his job to bring the ball downcourt. The Banshees were poised with all their speed on defense.

They tried to pin him to the sideline. He had learned the answer to that one. He spun around, changing hands. He lost his man. He went over the line. The Banshees faltered and he saw Charlie Mount looming. He slammed the pass. Mount took it and dunked it.

The score became Banshees one hundred, Beavers ninety-nine. The clock was menacing the trailing team. The Beavers had to go man for man and try to get back the ball without utilizing the intentional foul tactic.

Jordan suddenly went into swift action. He waved one hand in the face of the Beaver guard and reached with the other. The man turned and Krash was on the spot. Krash knocked the ball loose.

Don saw it coming. Anticipating the play he took the ball in stride and dribbled low and hard. Jordan was yelling to him that he was loose but Don saw his lane. He ran into it.

He jumped to make his shot. He was fouled. The ball went through for two points to finally put the Beavers ahead.

Don stood on the black line. He was trembling with excitement. He steadied himself. He made the free throw high and easy. It came down like a nesting bird. It sank through the net. The score became Beavers 102, Banshees 100.

Reed called for time and inserted his first string. Don went to the bench. He was slapped on the back until he lost his breath. Reed was grinning like the fabled Cheshire cat. On the court Alcorn, Farber, Krash and Mount were passing the ball around. The Banshees had to go for the intentional foul. Alcorn sank it. Before the Banshees could get the play going the horn sounded to end the game and the Beavers had put away their very first win in a new season in a new town in a new auditorium.

The Hall family was screaming itself hoarse. As Don left the hall he saw Kitty and Homer for the first time, seated on high. They were applauding and waving at him. The crowd was going crazy. Tomorrow there would be another good turnout, he thought. Nothing could have been more exciting than the debut of the Beavers.

In the dressing room Beans Jordan was frowning. He said, "You know, Don, you're supposed to pass to the open man. That's what the boss man says. Well, I was wide open when you went in that last time."

"Tough, man, tough," Alcorn told him. "Don saw his way. He had a layup."

"Well, how does this team play it?" demanded Jordan. "Tell me one thing—then do another. How about it?"

Reed spoke, for the first time his voice harsh, commanding. "Brand was right. His shot was dead-sure."

"You think I ever miss from fifteen, twenty feet?" demanded Jordan. "I just dɔn't get it, is all. One way or the other, that's the way it's got to be."

Reed said coldly, "It's going to be my way. Get that straight, Jordan. My way!"

For a moment it seemed as if Beans was going to fight back. Then he made a chameleonlike change. He grinned, shrugged, spread his long arms. "Like I say. The boss man is always right."

He went to his locker and began to strip. Reed remained standing, squared away, looking at the players. "Any questions?"

Alcorn said, "Not from me."

"I notice you're not elated by the win tonight," said Reed. "You're right. You shouldn't be. If we don't do better we can forget about the playoffs. You all know that."

Alcorn said, "We know it."

Reed relaxed. "Okay. It's a good opening game. The crowd here is not yet basketball-hip. We'll try and put it all together as we go along. That's all I have to say."

"It's enough," Alcorn replied.

The team went on about the business of bathing and dressing. It was quiet in the locker room. Don Brand was thoughtful.

He had done well, he believed. He should not have passed off to Beans Jordan when he knew his lane was open to the basket. He felt that Reed's system was correct and he had followed it to the limit of his capability. His only doubt was whether he had enough skill and muscle and durability to improve and be of real value as the long season continued.

He went out of the hall and found Martha waiting. He was conscience-stricken, for he had actually forgotten their date.

He said, "Hey, I'm sorry I took so long. The coach—you know."

"Sure, I know." She was bright and smiling. "Pa and the boys just left. They said to tell you how great you were. But you already know."

They went to his car. He said, "Not great. Just beginning." He could talk to her, tell her all about it because she was in the basketball scene and she understood. They drove to Ventura Boulevard and went into the Tail o' the Cock and ordered a big meal.

Later he wondered about Kitty McCoy and Homer and what they were doing. His mind was filled with a number of things . . .

The next night the Banshees destroyed the Beavers, 105 to 86.

6

Amazingly, unbelievably, the season was almost over. The Beavers sat in the dressing room of Madison Square Garden in New York and nursed their wounds. They had just lost the second game of a twin series with the Knicks.

But they had won the first game, Don Brand assured himself. They had also split with the Bullets the previous two nights. They had been on a long and murderous road trip and they had managed to stay atop the weak Western Division.

Now they had to fly back West and play the Jaybirds in the northwest town which was the home of Killer Kane's team. It was, by the vagaries of scheduling, their first series against the leaders of the Midwest Division. It was another idiosyncrasy of basketball that the Jaybirds were placed in the Midwest, which they led by a vast margin. Indeed there were experts who were saying that the trade between the Beavers and Jaybirds had put new life into Killer Kane and probably handed the national title to the team from Northwest City.

Whereas the Beavers had profited nil by acquiring Beans Jordan, so the story went in newspapers and magazines. Don sat and listened to the coach. Hobie Reed was as finely drawn and gaunt as his worn-down players.

Reed said, "You've done as well as can be expected. These long trips are worse than anyone suspects until he's been on one. I know you're all hurting. It's astounding we haven't had more serious injuries."

"It's the only reason we're on top in our division," said Bud Alcorn flatly.

"Maybe. But we're improved," Reed said.

"Some of us," said Charlie Mount, staring at Beans Jordan.

The veterans would never adjust to the free-wheeling shooter, Don knew. And it seemed Beans would never make a real effort to play Hobie Reed's game. It was the one flaw in the slow building of the Beavers.

Bud Alcorn removed the bandage from his knee. The scars of surgery were plainly visible. The swelling and discoloration were blue and black and green.

He said, "I think we go ahead. I think we keep doing our thing."

"You've got a night off. The flight's at noon tomorrow. We don't play until the following day which is a big break. Go out and relax and have fun," said Hobie Reed. "You deserve a good time."

"I'm too old and too tired to have a good time," said Alcorn. He grinned. "But I can sure sleep up a storm."

They dressed and went to the midtown hotel where they were quartered. There were two airmail-special letters for Don. When he got upstairs his roomie was already changing to bright, gay raiment. Beans was limping around but he was beaming. He waved and spoke happily.

"Come on, let's hit the town."

"I haven't got the strength, man," said Don. He flopped on the bed and opened the first letter.

It was from Martha Hall. It was full of breezy, offhand comments from the family, all about basketball and the hometown gossip. It ended, "Things are not so good at the office. Your father seems kind of disinterested lately. Kitty is uptight about something. But I stay on, I like the company and the people. . . . Wish you were here as they say on the postcards . . . I really miss you . . . Love, Martha."

Beans said, "Look, I can dig up a couple of chicks and we can make the scene, man. You never seen New York till you seen it with me."

"I'll bet," said Don. He ripped open the letter from Kitty McCoy.

"Dearest Don: You were right. No sense of humor. Your father is also lacking in that department lately. Hurry home and console me. . . . Love, Kitty."

He said, "Oh, boy!"

Beans said, "Look, you can't let me hit the big time alone. I got enough trouble. With you along everything is bound to be copascetic, right?

Don consulted his watch. It was eleven o'clock. It would be eight at home in California. He picked up the room phone and made a collect call to his home.

Beans said, "We can sleep in the morning. Just a couple hours, roomie? Pretty please?"

The voice of Brand, Sr. came on the wire. "Hello . . . Junior?"

"Who else dares call collect? How are you, father?"

"Why, fine. Perfectly fine. How are you?"

"Tired but healthy thus far. It's been a rough trip."

"So I gather from Martha. She keeps me in touch."

"I'm sorry about that. I don't have time to breathe, much less write. I should call more often."

"Quite all right. I understand."

"You don't sound very enthusiastic."

"About basketball? I'm not, you know."

"About anything. You sure you're all right?"

"Of course."

"Things going well at the company?"

"As usual." Now there was a toneless quality to the voice of Brand, Sr.

"Look, I'll be home next week and we'll have dinner and a talk. Okay?"

"That will be very nice."

"You sure you're okay?"

"Just fine," said his father.

"Well . . . good-bye."

"Good night, Junior."

Don hung up. There was something definitely different—wrong—about his father. The two letters, the intonations of the voice, were not as they should be.

Then the girls, that budding problem, struck at him. Both of them signed "love." Both looked forward to having him come home and comfort them. Homer Sanders had evidently fouled out. Martha . . . he always felt warm when he thought of Martha and her family.

His mind boggled. There was no time in his life at

present to think of anything but basketball. It was difficult indeed to hang on and be useful to the team. He had been too often confused and baffled by canny opponents—he had still a long, long way to go before he could call himself a real pro. He felt he was growing, finding himself but the process was too slow.

Beans said, "You never even seen New York."

Don brought his mind to the present problem. "You're double trouble, Beans."

"Now, just because of that little old thing in Baltimore, don't get me wrong."

"A burleycue queen, no less."

"Well, she was okay."

"What about her friend?"

"She wasn't okay," admitted Beans. "But this is different. Let's just make the scene, huh? No chicks."

"There's no way you can stay away from girls," Don said. "What about Alicia?"

"A nice kid," said Beans. "Real nice. But she ain't here, is she?"

It would be better to go with him, Don thought. In Baltimore there might have been real trouble if Beans had been alone with the alcoholic friend of his burlesque dancer and the rough element in the dive they had been led into. Also, he couldn't help his liking for his roomie. He did not believe there was a malicious thought in the kid's head. He was just a country boy upon whom riches had been poured and who could not quite understand his responsibilities.

He said, "Oh, all right. Let's make the scene."

He put on a sports coat and a tie. He followed the limping but ebullient Jordan out of the hotel. The noise and stench of New York hit him like a wave of dish water. But Beans was waving down a taxicab and he climbed in, barely able to fit in its mini-sized tonneau.

"The Four Trees," Beans said. "You know where it is?"

"Do I know my left elbow?" The cabbie squinted at them. "Basketball players. Were you lucky to take one from them Knicks, you bums."

"Yeah, we know," said Beans. "Get goin', man, it's later than you think."

The cabby rammed uptown a block, then wheeled around a corner eastward almost knocking down a scurrying pedestrian. He said, "I seen you win the game last night. Dumb luck. What are you gonna do against them Jaybirds, huh? No way. That Killer Kane I wish we had him. He's moider."

"We're scared to pieces," said Beans.

"You better be. He got new life. When you mugs traded him it made him sore or somethin'. It's either them or the Knicks, you better believe it."

"They beat the Knicks two games."

"I seen 'em when they done it. Moider, I says."

"We read the papers."

"You ain't met 'em yet. They got that Moe Drabski, he come from here. Uptown, the playgrounds, along with Handy Eller and Billy Arnold."

"Bud Alcorn and Charlie Mount came from there, too," said Don.

"Uh-huh. Old men. . . . Them Jaybirds also got Cal Carr. When you seen him you seen somethin' fast. And tough. They're all rough, gutsy guys. They'll moralize you bums."

"We'll survive," said Don, restraining Beans.

"With sore shins," said the cabby. "They're perzon."

Beans yelled, "You wanna bet?"

The cabdriver sneered. "You make a bet—you're outa basketball. Don't you know that yet a'ready?" He peered into the mirror. He chuckled on an evil key. "Oh, sure. You that hillbilly kid they traded Kane for. Ha, ha, ha, ha!"

Beans said, "Stop this crate. Lemme outa here. I'll tear him apart."

The cabby pulled to the curb. He got out and held a spanner at his side. "You wanna make somethin' out of it you got the right guy, bum."

Don sighed, interposing his length between them, proffering a bill. "Forget it."

"He wanted to bet. He could be barred for life for wantin' to make a bet," shouted the cabby.

Don said to Beans, "Beat it. Quick."

"I'll beat him!" Beans tried to get past Don.

The cabby said, "Let him come. I'll bust his skull in."

Don thrust the bill into the cabdriver's pocket. He gave him a deft shove. People were staring, but thanks to the New York disinclination to get involved they were not approaching. The cabby stumbled in the gutter.

Don grabbed Beans and rushed him around a corner. He yanked him into a narrow alleyway and said, "Now hold still before I clobber you myself."

In a minute or two the cab came cruising down the street in search of them. After he had passed Don pulled Beans back toward Third Avenue.

"That was a determined character," Don observed.

"I'd a fixed his wagon."

"Sure, you would. And you'd be on the front pages tomorrow. Have you any other place than our destination in mind?"

"What?"

"Our cabdriver will be checking your Four Trees. He not only dislikes you personally, he's a Knicks fan. He'd love to make a fuss."

"I didn't make any bet. I just. . . ."

"You just sounded off." Don began walking back toward the hotel where they were staying.

"Well, who's goin' to take that kind of stuff?"

"Like the man who was kicked by the mule—you have to consider the source."

"I just can't be like you." Beans was suddenly subdued, keeping step with his companion along the narrow New York street. "I guess you're right—most of the time."

"I don't want to be right. I just want to be safe," said Don. "Haven't we got problems enough?"

"We got the division title sewed up. People worry too much." Already his spirits were returning. "If Reed would only turn me a-loose more, open up the game."

Don sighed. "Let's stop some place and get a beer," he said. "Only don't bet the bartender, will you?"

Beans said, "Hey, I know where we are now. There's a nice place on Lexington. Picked up a swell chick there last time I was in New York . . . or was that next to last time?"

"I wasn't with you," said Don. "And please, no chicks."

"You don't dig broads much, do you?"

"If you only knew," said Don.

Coach Reed was the last one on the plane. The Beavers occupied the entire first-class cabin of the Boeing 707. He came in with his brow furrowed, his mouth grim.

They took off. The curtain was drawn between first and second class. The movie screen came down. The coach put up a hand and said, "Don't adjust your earphones. Listen to me."

They listened. He stood in the aisle. He pointed a finger at the seats occupied by Don and Beans Jordan.

"What about last night?"

"Oh-oh," said Beans.

"The cabdriver," said Don.

"I had a call from the commissioner. It was reported that Jordan offered to bet we would beat the Jaybirds tomorrow night."

"It's not true," said Don.

"Then it was you who were with him?"

"That's right. We went out for a beer and a sandwich," said Don. "The taxi driver got tough. Beans just answered him—it was a manner of answering. That's all."

"You mean Jordan just said, 'I'll betcha,' something like that?"

"He said, precisely, 'You wanna bet?' Then the driver threatened us."

"Did you attack him?"

"He offered to attack us. With a wrench."

"You didn't hit him?"

"I would've," interjected Beans. "Don wouldn't let me."

"That I believe," said Reed. "I also believe Don. But before you can play, Jordan, we'll have to make a statement for the commissioner."

"You mean I'm suspended?" demanded Beans. "On the word of that dumb-bunny cabdriver I'm suspended?"

"Pending a statement."

"That means I'll miss the first game!"

"Yes. That's what it means. The commissioner has to be one hundred per cent careful. You all know the problem. If there's ever a hint of a gambling scandal the pro game goes out the window the way the college game did a few years ago."

Don said, "It's damned unfair."

"That may be. But that's the way it is," said Reed.

Charlie Mount said, "I knew his big mouth would get us in trouble sooner or later."

"It was not his fault this time," Don said quickly. "Anyone would have resented the way the cabby behaved."

"You took his jive," said Mount. "How come you didn't get on him?"

"It's not my bag," said Don. "But I can't blame Beans."

"Stickin' up for your roomie." Mount's grievance had been growing for some time. "Two whiteys go out and cause trouble."

Bud Alcorn spoke from a rear seat. "That's enough, Charlie."

"You, too. My own cousin. You know damn well this team would be better off without that hillbilly mushmouth. And now he's got his roomie on his side."

Coach Reed's voice was low but sharp, commanding. "I've heard enough."

"You haven't heard anything," Mount began.

Alcorn interrupted. "You heard the coach. Shut up!"

Sam Felton said, "Now wait. Charlie's right. We could have traded for Cat Ballew instead of the flake, here. He's had his chance and he's still a showboat."

"Looks like this club wants more whiteys than soul brothers," Mount said. "Look at the champions. Mostly black men."

It was out in the open, Don thought. There had been an undercurrent but he had thought it was solely against Jordan. He looked to Coach Reed.

Alcorn said in his deep voice, "You cats are dead wrong. No matter how you cut it, this club's straight. Every man gets his chance. Every man's got his place in the scheme of things. If you make trouble, then it's your red wagon."

Hobie Reed was facing them, his jaw muscles working, a slight flush upon his cheeks. His voice was heavy with feeling.

"As you know it's never been my way to take a hard line with you men. I believe a coach should guide his players, reason with them as adults. I've had the good advice and support of Bud which has helped. Now I'm going to tell you what the Lord told John." He took a deep breath. "Charlie, as Bud says, is dead wrong. We're in this game not only for the money. We're in it because of pride. Pride goes with accomplishment. We've built a pretty good team. If we're going anyplace every one of you must contribute above and beyond his ability. You can't do that if you're harboring rancor. Now I'll lay it out for you: if Charlie and Sam and whoever else is not ready to give—you can sit it out. I'll go with five men who have desire. I don't care who they are if they want to play the game. Do you get that?"

There was a silence. Beans Jordan moved restlessly alongside Don, who nudged him to silence. A stewardess started to come between the curtains, stopped and retreated. Bud Alcorn's fine features seemed carved in brown stone. The plane flew above a sea of fleecy white clouds.

Peanuts Hopwood said quietly, "Charlie wasn't talkin' for me, neither."

"Any questions?" Hobie Reed threw the words at them as though they were bullets.

Charlie Mount mumbled, "I didn't mean nothin' personal. Red, Johnny, George, Ed . . . they're buddies. I thought Brand was one of us till he got with the flake."

"The flake?" Reed was cold and steady. "That's a personal remark, Charlie."

"Well . . . okay. I take it back."

It was lukewarm but Don stuck an elbow in Jordan's ribs. Beans said, "It's okay, coach. Maybe I am a flake. Like Don says, I do attract trouble like a honey pot attracts flies. I should've kept my mouth shut last night."

"Is that good enough for you men?" demanded Reed.

"Well . . . sure. I mean . . . well, he means good. He never dogs it," Charlie Mount said painfully. "He just don't play our game, is all."

"*My* game," Reed pointed out. "And I'll be the judge."

"Well, sure. I mean, you're the coach." Charlie had settled into a low key.

"Jordan can shoot rings around any of you," Reed told

them. "He sits on the bench. You know why. He knows why. When he learns his lesson he'll be in the game more often. Is that understood by all of you?"

"It better be," said Bud Alcorn. "It just better be."

For the rest of the flight there was untoward silence in the first cabin. Each man had some thinking to do. Don spoke in low tones to Beans.

"You did right, roomie."

"I didn't know they hated me." Jordan was hurt and confused. "I reckon I don't think anybody hates me."

"Nobody does," Don assured him.

Beans shook his head. He was utterly unlike his usual bubbling self all the way to Northwest City. The surface had been smoothed over but there would be scars. An undercurrent still ran, possibly not strong, but ever present.

The Northwest City hall was not as spacious as the Garden or the Canyon City auditorium but it was jammed to capacity with rooters for the Jaybirds. The place vibrated with the spirit they engendered. It was different from other crowds, for these were new fans who understood little basketball but could thrill to the rough, muscular play of the home team.

The cabdriver had been right—they were big and strong and devil-may-care, Don knew. Billy Arnold and Handy Eller, the forwards, bore scars of combat. Both were shooters. Moe Drabski, the center, was almost as tall as Bud Alcorn and twice as aggressive in his attacks upon the opposition. Cal Carr was smaller but mean as a snake. And then there was Killer Kane.

Kane had pulled them together. Coach Grimm was an opportunist who knew when he had something going for him, which was to let Kane more or less direct the game pattern. The result was a team which had run away from the others in the Midwest Division and were favored to win the initial playoff and go into the finals.

The Beavers would have to play the Banshees in their first playoff. Don fully believed the Beavers could win. But the Jaybirds for the championship—that was another matter. Only time could give an indication—time and this present two-game duel.

Both teams had come thus far without serious injury. This was a huge factor over the long, hard season. Right now the Beavers were coming off the arduous long road trip and the Jaybirds had the advantage of the home court. All these factors had to be taken into consideration.

The warm-up finished, the Beavers went to the bench. The starters removed their jackets and the squad formed a huddle.

Coach Reed said, "This is the big test. One thing: don't let them make you change our game. No matter the score. Stay with it. Win or lose, don't break the pattern."

Alcorn said, "No way, coach. I been there before with the tough guys. No way."

"I don't need to tell you to watch the fouls. That's part of their thing," said Reed.

"Don't smack anybody," said Alcorn, grinning. "Not even the Killer."

"Especially not Kane," said Reed. "Let him get in foul trouble. He can do it."

It sounded grim and Don thought it most probably would be. He took his accustomed seat on the bench. He missed Beans, who was not in uniform. The statement had been made and was in the hands of the commissioner. The vindictive cabdriver had made one serious error, Hobie Reed was confident: he had not accused Don Brand in any fashion. Vindication was almost assured, the coach felt.

However the wire services had picked up the story from the cabby and the local papers had seized upon it with glee. Beans had never been popular in Northwest City and the reporters had a field day, assuming that he was guilty, abusing him for his eccentricities, maligning his ability, crowing over the trade which had brought Killer Kane to their team.

The game was about to begin when the hullabaloo started at the gate and spread so that the referee scowled and held the ball. The fans howled like banshees, "There he is, the gambler!" "Wanna bet, Beansy-boy?" "Tweaky ole Beans the betcha kid."

On the bench Hobie Reed said, "I advised him to stay in his room and watch on TV."

"I left him there intending to do just that," Don replied.

He came wearing a powder-blue suit with wide lapels and a white shirt ruffled with lace. He walked smiling through the inimical, jeering crowd. He found a seat directly in back of Don on the bench and said, "I gotta give you moral support, team."

Reed said, "We appreciate it a lot!"

"Let 'em howl," Beans said. "Tomorrow they can howl louder. But they'll buy tickets."

There was no gainsaying him, Don thought. It would sell tickets. It was show business. On the court Killer Kane was staring at the Beaver bench with his strange, pale eyes. To Kane it was not a show it was a war.

Sam Felton grumbled, "He shoulda stood in bed. Now they got something to really yell about."

Coach Reed said crisply, "Pay attention to the game."

"What game?" asked Felton.

The referee had hesitated too long. A crumpled program came down and hit Beans on the head. He caught it, turned and bowed in the direction from which it had come. It was immediately followed by a paper cup full of soft drink. This missed Beans and splattered the Beaver bench.

Hobie Reed was on his feet in an instant, hands raised. The officials came toward him. Uniformed guards and two policemen charged into the crowd. Bedlam reigned.

Reed said, "We can't play under these conditions."

The referee said, "Then get Jordan out of here."

"Not on your life. He has a right here."

"You're creating a disturbance by having him here."

"What disturbance has he created? Either control the crowd or I'm pulling out under protest," said Reed.

"How you can stand up for that flake I don't understand," said the official.

"If you'd started the game the crowd would have been watching it," Hobie Reed said forcefully. "Either handle the game or I'll call the commissioner."

"You're already in trouble with him." But the official went to the microphone and made the announcement that either the crowd would simmer down or the game was postponed. The guards and the police continued their efforts. In five minutes the mob had subsided except for occasional catcalls.

Killer Kane watched it all with disdainful mien, Don noted. He was like a jungle animal awaiting his chance to pounce. The referee took the ball back to the center of the court. The Beavers and Jaybirds jockeyed for position.

The ball went up. The two giant centers climbed the ozone. Bud Alcorn tipped the ball. It went back to Farber who dribbled for the right sideline and diagonally for the basket.

Killer Kane came crashing over. Peanuts Hopwood was in the path of the charging Jaybird guard. They came together. Peanuts went down writhing in pain.

Hobie Reed and the trainer rushed onto the court. Kane was laughing. No foul was called since there was no apparent reason to believe an intentional was committed . . . no reason so far as the officials were concerned. But Don Brand, shucking his jacket, knew better. Everyone on both benches knew Kane was out to get his former teammates.

Peanuts was helped off the court. The trainer took him to the dressing room. Hobie Reed's face was taut with rage as he looked at Don.

"He'll be after you twice as hard. Try to keep out of his way when you can."

Don said, "I'm not running from him."

Beans called from behind the bench, "Go get the bum, roomie. Show him what tough is."

"With Jordan out—be careful," Reed insisted.

"Yes, sir," said Don. He went into the game. He was seething with anger. Peanuts was the happy one, the veteran everyone liked.

It was Beavers' ball in-bounds. Don faked, then gave it to Red Farber and went down the court. He knew the pattern should be to the right and ran a semi-circle for deception. Kane, anticipating the play based on his experience as a Beaver, was right there. Alcorn assumed the low post and Farber gave to the center, thus breaking the pattern as Reed had indicated should be done occasionally against Kane's team.

Don went into the right corner. Alcorn spun and lofted

a pass to him. Don jumped. He took the shot. It went through to give the Beavers the first two points of the game.

Carr put it in play beneath the basket, giving to Kane. The strong-driving guard went dribbling away like an automaton. Don went with him.

They were neck and neck across the black line as the rest of the Beavers went into their positions on defense. Kane tried to race away. Don increased his pace, reaching for the ball, putting a hand before Kane's eyes.

Kane passed off. Immediately, as soon as attention was directed elsewhere, Don felt the now familiar elbow in his ribs.

Kane growled, "You're going to pay the price, rich kid. What I did to Peanuts is nothin'."

Don snapped back. "You try it and I'll give you worse than a duckin' in a fountain, you jerk."

He thought he saw the pale eyes blink in surprise at his quick rejoinder but he could not be sure. Kane was all fighter. His disposition was bad and his manners worse but that he was a great battler could not be denied. They went into the play together. The ball was passed to Kane.

Don swarmed him. Farber came over to help. Kane got rid of the ball to Drabski, his big center, another wild man with free-swinging elbows. Alcorn and Drabski clashed in the lane. Both men crashed to the floor. Don saw blood on Bud's lip.

The referee called the foul on the Beavers.

Drabski went to the line. He seemed a bit groggy but he managed to convert the foul.

The gorge rose in Don. He had always been slow to anger but again something was happening inside him, deep in his soul. It had all begun with Killer Kane, he thought, back in the game at the company gymnasium. It had been growing without his full knowledge.

He put the ball in play to Farber. Bud was moving on his storklike legs. Don ran past him, watching for Kane. Bud took the high post.

Don ran in front of Kane. He felt the impact of the knees and fists of the Killer. He bent low and Kane ran over him but staggered. Don went for the basket.

Bud had the ball. He turned and handed it off. The hole left by Kane's inability to regain balance was open. Don went in and laid up the ball. Drabski's arm slashed across his face. No harm, no foul, the officials always decided, but now there was blood inside Don's mouth.

The score was Beavers four, Jaybirds one. Killer Kane brought the ball along the court. Don covered him. Kane backed and dribbled, giving Don his hips. Don spun around him and slapped at the ball. Farber grabbed it and passed to Krash.

Krash scored over Cal Carr. It became six to one for the Beavers and now the tone of the crowd changed, became querulous as the inexperienced fans became restless.

One voice rose above the hum of discontent. Beans Jordan howled, "Take it to 'em, Beavers! Down their throats!"

The Beavers took it to them. They went into a man for man. They pushed and they shoved. The officials began to call fouls at last.

The score mounted. Don was playing in a red cloud. He kept as close to Kane as a porous plaster. He took the elbows and the digging fists and the clutches at his trunks. He gave it back as best he could. The first half went by in a blur of furious physical action.

The scoreboard read Beavers fifty-eight, Jaybirds forty-seven.

In the dressing room Beans Jordan was everywhere. His light-blue suit was splattered, his hair uncombed and wild. He hovered over Peanuts. The knee of the veteran guard was swollen; he would not play again in this series.

Beans said, "We'll get it back for you. We'll show 'em how to play that game."

Hobie Reed did not interfere. The coach was not about to hinder a team riding high on anger and the desire to win, Don thought admiringly. None of the Beavers had less than three personals—a bad situation but comparable to that of the Jaybirds in that department.

The coach asked quietly, "How do you feel, Don?"

"I can go."

"Ed Carey will relieve you when the time comes."

"I know. But I'd like to stay in as long as possible."

"Right," said Reed. He said very little more during the intermission. Bud Alcorn had a cut inside his mouth which needed attention, as did Don. The trainer swabbed. The players sat and talked quietly among themselves.

"Carry it right at 'em," Beans kept saying. "The only way to handle tough guys. Right at 'em."

"What's got into him?" Charlie Mount asked wonderingly.

Don said, "Team spirit. Ever hear of it?"

"Not from him."

Don's voice became sharp. "Take what's given to you, man."

Mount regarded him. "Seems like you got your dauber up, too."

"I haven't seen you on the floor as yet."

The big forward said softly, "I been knockin' my guy down."

"That's what I like to hear."

The signal was given and they went out to fight the Jaybirds hand to hand. It was like a free-for-all, Don thought. The officials were fair and willing but the fouls were committed cannily so that they were not always apparent.

The second half was a repetition of the first. Whistles blew, foul shots were made—and missed. Long before time was running out Kane, Alcorn, Mount and Farber were in foul trouble, as were Drabski and Handy Eller, the Jaybird forward.

The Jaybirds had to substitute with the score Beavers ninety, home team eighty. The continuous fouling had kept the score low. Hobie Reed removed Don from the game.

The coach said, "Take deep breaths. Relax. This is the longest you've ever played for us."

Don said, "If Kane goes back in—I want him."

"You've taken good care of him," said Reed warmly.

"Funny thing. A guy like that lifts you above your game."

"He's poison, all right."

Beans was leaning over them from behind. "What do

they call it? Anecdote? Antidote? Don's got it, whatever it is."

Billy Arnold, the remaining first-string Jaybird forward, was getting hot. The score became Beavers ninety-two, Jaybirds eighty-eight.

Don moved uneasily. Then he saw Kane getting ready to return to the game. He jumped up and took off his jacket. He would never before have anticipated the coach's wishes in this fashion. It was a night when the rules went out the window.

Reed said, "Go in for Carr. Just hold them. There's only a few moments left. Play it tight."

Alcorn also went into the game. The Beavers had the signal. Defense, defense, which was their game, was the answer to the present situation.

They played it that way. Into the game plan charged Killer Kane with five fouls on him. His skill was uncanny, Don had to admit. When he wanted to play the game as it should be played he was superb. He stole the ball at once and went for the basket.

Don got in his way. Kane faked, then went right. Don followed him, ignoring the feint. Kane tried to shoot over him. Don jumped high. His fingers touched the ball.

Alcorn was there. The center stuck out his elbows and rotated the ball until the defense was ready. The Beavers went down the court and passed for twenty-three seconds. Then Alcorn passed off to Don.

Kane was atop him, sticking a hand in his face. Don bounced the ball once and slung it underhand toward the basket. It caromed off the board. Alcorn went high. Bud's fingers caressed the leather. The ball went in for two points.

That was the end. The Jaybirds scored to make it ninety to ninety-four but there was not enough time for further play.

The Beavers had won their first contest in the crucial match of the year.

Killer Kane said to Don, "You're over your head, rich kid. Way over your head. You know it, too."

"Thanks," Don told him. "You do that for me, tough cat. Try me again, any time."

Kane's fist clenched. Then he narrowed his pale eyes and said, "I promise." Then he walked away.

Don had never known complete exhaustion before. The road trip, the flight, then this game had drained him. He was lying on his bed in a half stupor when Beans crashed into the room.

Beans chortled, "Hobie got a call. The cabby cracked. They give him the third degree and he finked. Told the damn truth. I get to play tomorrow."

"You're real excited about it, aren't you?"

Beans sat down. "You know what? I never been so excited. You cats did such a tremendous job. I mean tremendous! It got me all stirred up."

"It got me all worn down," said Don. "Can we just take it nice and easy tonight?"

"Well, I know this chick, see? From when I was playin' here. Promised to buy her a drink."

"Oh, great!"

"But I'll make curfew tonight. You wait and see."

He did, too. He wakened Don to prove it. Don groaned and then tossed and turned for an hour before he could get back to sleep again.

The following night in the dressing room the Beavers received the bad news about Peanuts Hopwood. The ligaments in his knee were gone, and required surgery—the second time for him, probably a sign he would never play again. It was not what he meant on the court, Don knew, it was that he had been the cheerful one, the happy member under all circumstances.

The anger was deep. Peanuts had been fouled. There was little conversation among the players. Even Beans was quiet.

The fans were also subdued. Don was to start—he had definitely passed the veteran Carey for position on the squad, it seemed. They took the court.

Kane was without words as they began. His pale eyes no longer glared; they were narrowed in concentration. The Jaybirds did not attack with ferocity.

Don found himself in an entirely different game. The

Killer directed a diversified attack. Drabski did not challenge Bud Alcorn. There were no arrant fouls.

The Jaybirds were a smooth, swift machine. They played like champions. Overnight they had pulled themselves together. Kane led them all the way.

The Jaybirds won the game, 102 to 94. Only great outside shooting by Beans Jordan, subbing for Don Brand, had kept the score that close.

And Killer Kane had a word for Don. "One minute of glory, rich kid. You had it. It's over. I only hope you make the playoffs. You cats will be a lead-pipe cinch."

7

Don Brand was the last to leave the airplane at Los Angeles. He groaned as he lifted down his suitcase, and limped toward the exit. The weight of the long road trip and the two games in Northwest City against the Jaybirds were upon him. Every muscle in his body ached. His ears buzzed from decompression because the plane had descended a bit too quickly. He had never felt worse.

The wives and children were on hand to greet the weary homecoming warriors. Bud Alcorn picked up one of his cousin's kids and held him squealing, delighted, aloft. Beans Jordan walked into the widespread arms of Alicia Aster and danced off, limping only a little, toward the parking lot. The Reed family swarmed upon the coach.

Don was half-asleep by the time he reached the crowd. He came wide awake when he saw those waiting for him.

Martha Hall was with her father. Beyond her was Kitty McCoy. Panic began to stir in Don's middle.

Martha reached him first, hugged him. "We saw the game. Both games. You were wonderful . . . we're so sorry about Peanuts, though . . . how are you? Are you all right?"

"Fine, fine," he said. He saw Kitty's small smile a few feet away.

"We came to drive you home," Martha said.

Pat Hall came forward and offered his hand. "Good games," he said. "That's a tough team, the Jaybirds."

"Real tough," said Don. He could not take his eyes away from Kitty. He had no idea how he was going to handle this situation. He had never in his life been met by two girls. "It's awful nice for you to meet me."

"You look so tired," said Martha with concern. "We'll take you right home."

"Uh—well, fine," said Don. Kitty had that knowing little half smile on her face. She looked mighty pretty, too. He scratched his weary brain for what to do next.

"Well, come on," said Martha, tugging at his hand.

"Uh . . . just a minute." They evidently didn't know Kitty was behind them. He drew a deep breath. "There's—uh—someone . . ."

At that moment his father came into view. Brand, Sr. had been standing in back of the tall Kitty. He lifted one hand and called, "Junior!"

Martha and her father turned. They saw Don's father and blinked.

Don said, "I'll be darned. Imagine him coming all the way over here to meet the plane!"

"And Kitty." Martha had lost her smile of welcome.

"Yeah, well, you see, father doesn't drive well at night. Uh—I guess I'll have to ride with them." He recovered himself, drawing a breath. "How about tomorrow, Martha? Call you?"

"I'll be working," she said. Her smile returned. "I'm glad your father came to get you. He's been—well, I'm glad."

"Yeah, the old man's been peaked lately," Pat Hall said bluntly. "Funny, though. He called me, asked me some basketball questions."

"He did what?" Don couldn't believe his ears.

"Pretty smart questions, too," said Pat Hall. "Okay, Don, See you later."

They moved away. Don went to Kitty and his father. He said, "This is a surprise."

"Thought you might need a ride," said his father. "Was that Martha Hall?"

"Yes. She thought the same thing." He looked at Kitty. "Thanks for the letter, Kitty. Good to see you."

"Think nothing of it," she said. Her voice was cool and controlled but the little smile remained.

"Kitty brought her own car. Thought we might have coffee or something." Brand, Sr. seemed a bit flustered. "We saw the games together. She explained a lot to me."

They walked toward the exit. Don was puzzled.

"Kitty explained basketball?"

"We've been studying," Kitty said. "Books, you know?"

"Basketball books?"

"The one your coach wrote," said Mr. Brand. "Too complicated. Takes an expert to understand it."

"I see." It was a revelation, all right. "Well, maybe you ought to see some games."

"Yes," said his father. "I've been having a bit of brain lag, the doctor tells me. Too much company, too many hours concentrating on business. I've turned over some of the work to a new department under Sanders. You remember Homer Sanders."

"Oh, yes. I remember him," said Don. He glanced at Kitty. The smile had vanished.

"He has executive ability," said Mr. Brand. "Not a great engineer, you understand. But he takes over."

"That's just fine," said Don. "Look, why don't we go to my place and let me change and then sit around a while?"

"I'd like that," said his father.

Kitty said nothing. She drove them to the apartment in her swift and efficient style. She dutifully came in and waited while Don made instant coffee and talked with his father about the trip, about the tough games in Northwest City, about the plane rides and the meals at difficult hours and the physical strain of the professional game. She offered nothing in the way of contribution to the discourse, sipping the coffee, regarding Don with a reflective gaze.

They were leaving when she said, "You look different, somehow, Don. Older, maybe."

"Maybe I am older." He returned her level glance.

"Experience of all kinds is valuable," his father said. "I've thought a lot about it. That first game up north. That was very rough, was it not?"

"Very rough," said Don.

"You reacted to it. You became physical," said Brand, Sr. shrewdly. "Even I could detect it. That was an experience."

"You're right, sir."

"I don't know whether it's altogether good. It would be rather sad to find yourself brutalized, seeking combat."

"Yes. I agree with that," said Kitty. "Basketball was not conceived as a game of body contact."

"You've been reading the wrong books." Don grinned at them. "In the pro game it's contact and plenty of it. Just watch the play under the baskets."

His father said, "Why don't we have dinner after the game tomorrow night? I take it you dine after the game?"

"Yes, well . . . I'm sorry. I have a date."

"Oh. In that case, I'll wait to hear from you."

"I'll talk to you at the game. You are attending?" The exchange had become formal and Don did not know how to extricate himself. He was aware of Kitty's knowing gaze.

"Yes. I've decided to at least watch you play." But the warmth was gone, and his father was analyzing him again.

Kitty said, "Good night, Don. See you tomorrow, then."

They left. He felt deflated going back into the apartment, reaching for the yogurt and honey. Kitty had said he was different and he realized this was true. What he did not know was precisely in what way he had changed and whether it was for the better. He did know he was sore in every joint, that he was too tired to be at his physical peak for the upcoming games with the visiting Banshees.

He knew Beans Jordan was changing too. He was worried that the other men didn't seem to perceive this alteration in the wild young man. With Peanuts out for the season it was absolutely imperative that Beans fit into the pattern of the Beaver play. If he were not recognized as trying then he would rebel—that was his way of life.

He took his mixture of health food to the bedroom. He never did get it all down his throat. He fell asleep.

The music in the discotheque was deafening to Beans Jordan this particular night. He signed autographs for longhaired boys and girls, scarcely distinguishing one sex from the other, which was certainly unlike him. Alicia Aster danced with—or opposite to—a young actor of her acquaintance while Beans rested his aching leg. It was eleven o'clock and already he was stifling yawns.

Alicia returned to the tiny table. "Actors! He saw a producer and left me flat."

"Not flat," said Beans, eyeing her low-cut mini-outfit. "Hey, I'm hungry. You mind?"

"I don't mind anything, dearie," she said, smiling fondly upon him. "What you wanta do?"

"Let's mosey over to the other joint and grab a steak sandwich or somethin'."

"Why sure, honey." She was quickly solicitous, always agreeable. "Why didn't you say somethin'?"

"Because I'm not used to bein' hungry at this hour. That road trip was a scene. The game last night, they like to kill me."

"But you played good."

"You wouldn't know it if I did." He gimped across the mall to the restaurant. There were few customers inside. He escorted her to a booth and motioned to a waiter. He had learned how to manage in public in the past year. He was polite but firm ordering from the waiter. "You really don't catch on too good, angel, you know that."

"Sure. I know it." She smiled upon him. "But I saw you on the tube, runnin' and shootin' the ball and all that. You couldn't help it if your team lost."

"You keep on believin' that," he sighed. "Because I know better."

She said, "You know what, Beansy? You're not up tonight."

"Uh-huh." He was thinking of the way Killer Kane had roughed him on the court last night. It had been the worst of his many experiences in pro basketball. Yet Kane had not been detected, in fact had played a cleaner game than the night before against Don Brand. Kane was smart.

She said, "I mean, you're kind of down. I never saw you down before."

"How about that?" He could not concentrate on Alicia's dialogue. The food came. His appetite was good—it was his mind that wandered.

She said, "Beansy!"

"Oh . . . yeah?"

"Beansy—what's your regular first name? I mean, I never heard it."

"Oh. Oscar." He blinked. "What's your real name?"

She blushed. She drew a breath and whispered, "You won't ever tell anybody?"

"Why should I?" She had his attention now. She was a strange one, he thought, sometimes so Hollywood-wise, sometimes so innocent.

"Okay. It's Sophia."

"Sophia Aster?"

"Certainly not. Sophia Glotzman."

"Glotzman?"

"It's sort of Polish-Russian. But definitely Jewish."

"Jewish? How about that?"

"You keep saying 'how about that?' Like you're not really with it tonight."

"Oh, I'm with it tonight and all the time. But you got something on your mind, right?"

"Well, there's a producer. Manny Selman. Young fella."

"Uh-huh. I heard about him."

"Yes. He was talking. He said you and me, you know, we're a handsome couple."

"Smart man!"

"So he's got a story. One of those movies for television. It's a love story and a basketball story. I should ask you, he said. He might could use us."

"A movie?" Here it was, what he'd stored in the back of his mind all along. Hollywood, the silver screen, dreamland of his boyhood. Another step along the way to fame and glory and more money. The Beans Jordan story building to ultimate victory.

Alicia said, "If you want it, Beans. I mean I'm not pushing. I've got a job, right? A steady job."

"I'll talk to the guy." He knew what it meant to her, a chance to move above and beyond her small part in the series. He had meant to go home and rest his weary bones. But he finished his food and went with Alicia back to the discotheque.

Selman was of the new Hollywood breed, quick, smooth but without cant. He led them out to a bench on the mall.

"It's a notion," he said. "I happen to have a basketball

story. Tough, believe me. Vital. The nitty gritty. I can shoot it for peanuts. I got it sold to a network . . . if I have a Beans Jordan and a known gal like Alicia, here. We'd have to work fast, you know, while basketball is hot. If you agree, I'll go ahead tomorrow."

Beans asked, "When would it be done?"

"Well, not until after the season. But I'd need you for conferences, to show interest, make them know you're in." He looked at Alicia. "I have to tell you, there's a nude scene."

Beans spoke slowly, "A nitty-gritty story. A nude scene. I suppose the star's a crook?"

"A crook? Well, now, let's say he's an anti-hero. That's the scene nowadays. Nobody wants heroes, you know. He's like, he's a victim, see? They used him in college. The pros bought his body, right? That's what they do, you sign that contract and they own your body."

"Do tell," murmured Beans. His mind was off again, taking a trip back to college, to the contract and the money he had been given by the Jaybirds. "How about that?"

Alicia said, "Now, Beansy."

Manny Selman seemed disconcerted. "Well, it's true. Read the books coming out, the in-depth magazine stories. Sports is the bunk. Sports is a dying institution."

"You believe that?" asked Beans.

"Everybody knows it."

"And you want me to take time to sell your notion and work with it and I expect you want some expert advice?"

"Well, of course. You are a pro. You know the score."

Beans said, "I know the score? Look, man, I don't know your score. I mean, I don't dig, you know? I mean, sure I'd like to be in movies. I'd like Alicia to get a chance, a break. But, man, you've got the wrong kid."

"You haven't even heard about the money." Manny Selman smiled. "It's not chopped liver, you know."

Beans made an effort. "Look, I'm not puttin' down movies nor the loot, nor you. I appreciate the offer. Fact is, well, it's something I had in mind. Someday. But you forget, we got a chance for the national playoff."

"Oh?" Selman looked perplexed. "That's good? Or bad?"

"I'm on the team. The Beavers. If we make it we'll be on national TV, right?"

"Well, of course."

"And the publicity gets out. I'm doin' a nudie picture about a jerk basketball pro, right?"

"It's been done before by athletes."

"Yeah. I know. Bombed, too." Beans shook his head, wondering at himself. "Listen to me. Old flakey Beans. I'm sorry, Manny-boy. You're probably right. Not so long ago I'd have said you were right. But I can't do it."

The young producer looked at Beans, then he looked at Alicia. He spread his hands.

"What can I say? It was a notion."

"I hope you give Alicia a chance anyway."

Selman arose. "Sure. Sometime, something'll come along. She photographs." He paused, then went on, "You know something, Beans?"

"I ain't too sure I do."

"I think you're misunderstood. I see nothing flakey about you. Furthermore . . . you've got guts and you deserve credit."

Beans felt his cheeks glow. "Hey, man. This is all new stuff to me. Thanks a heap anyway."

Selman waved and walked back to the discotheque. Alicia put out a tentative hand.

"Beansy"

"I'm real sorry, Alicia."

"Beansy, I got to say I never heard you talk like that. I got to say it sounded wonderful."

"What's so wonderful?"

"I know you wanted to be in pictures. You told me once."

"I talk too much."

"Look, Beansy, we're young. We got careers ahead of us. I may be kind of dumb but I know what I've got and I know what you've got. We'll be all right."

He put his arm around her. "Baby, *you're* all right. You're really all right."

They sat for a while in peace, resting against each other.

Bud Alcorn told one last basketball story to the Reed kids, then helped put them to bed. He left them with their mother and came downstairs where Hobie sat in the den.

"You make this a home to me," Bud said. "You and Dorothy, you're too much."

"We got to know each other."

"Uh-huh. Interdependence of people . . . it's the big thing we miss most of the time." He eased himself into a chair. Out of his own home he had to be careful of furniture. He stretched his legs half across the room. "Now, about Peanuts."

"He's out," said Hobie Reed. "Definitely out."

"And Carey can't cut it."

"No, Carey is bench, just bench with muscles."

Bud mused, "This is purely something else. You treat me like a human being. I've been around a long time and all my coaches thought of me as a body. 'Difficult' they called me 'The big fellow' is hard to get along with."

"Why do you think I refused to hire an assistant coach?" Hobie asked quietly.

"Now I know."

"You're my assistant coach. Coming here to Canyon City, moving to an untried territory, taking over a club like the Beavers I had to depend on someone."

"So you traded Kane."

"He's not my kind of man."

"Neither is Beansy-boy."

"I don't know about him as yet."

Bud said, "Yeah. Right. The kid's got all kinds of guts."

"Beans and Don Brand. Too much depends on them. But that is what we have. What would you suggest?"

Bud said promptly, "Talk to them. Best thing is they get along together. I'd never have believed it but they do. Rooming them together was a great idea you had."

"What about cousin Charlie and Sam Felton?"

"Sad cats," said Bud promptly. "They got bees in their ears. But one thing can straighten them up quick."

"What's that?"

"Getting to the final playoff. They have families. The

big money means more to them than to me or Jordan or Brand."

"I see your point. Then we are right. It comes down to whether the two kids can pull us through the rest of the season and the preliminary playoff."

"The season we can manage. Then—who knows? Like you say, do the kids come through or not?"

Hobie said, "You see? We agree. It's that simple."

"Excuse me, Coach. Nothing's simple for a beat-up old dude over seven feet high." Bud smiled to take the solemnity from his words. "However—let's give it a try. Let's call that Beans cat."

Hobie looked at his watch. "It's only eleven. Maybe we could have a talk with him."

"He's the one. Don is okay."

"You're right." Hobie went to the phone. "Hate to wake up a player but this is important."

He dialed. He held the instrument to his ear while it rang six times.

He said sadly, "Out on the town again."

"Uh-huh. Are you surpised?"

"No. Disappointed. But not surprised."

"It's his style," said Bud Alcorn slowly. "On the court we might handle him. We might. Changing his style is another matter. Right?"

"Too right," agreed Hobie moodily. "Too damn right."

Beans Jordan parked the Maserati. He kissed Alicia good night. He saw her to her apartment door. He kissed her again. He had never experienced such a warmth toward anyone, certainly not even during his unhappy childhood.

He hurried to his apartment feeling virtuous. He unlocked the door, realizing that the telephone was ringing. Another one of those fans who somehow get hold of the number, he thought. He walked leisurely across the room and reached for the instrument. It stopped ringing before he could pick it up.

He yawned and looked at his watch. For once he was getting to bed on time, cold sober, getting his rest before a game. It was eleven o'clock.

It was spring time in the land and some thought of baseball but this did not include a single citizen of Northwest City. The final playoff was at hand. Killer Kane had led his team to the lopsided victories that gave the town the advantage of the odd games at home. Tickets were more precious than family heirlooms.

Furthermore the championship seemed a foregone conclusion for the Jaybirds. Their opponents were the Beavers.

Don Brand and Beans Jordan lounged in the motel room near the Northwest City auditorium and talked in low tones in which amazement and awe were equally mingled.

"I don't believe it," said Don. "On the other hand, it's been so long since the season opened that I can't remember it all."

"I knew it all the time," said Beans. "How could we lose with me shootin' for us?"

"You did fine," said Don. "You pulled us out of a lot of tough spots."

Beans dropped his air of lofty pretense. "Hey, man. We split time, remember? They told us we had to do it and we did it."

"I'm not a real pro, not yet," said Don. "Nobody knows it better than I do."

"You're good enough for me, roomie." Beans lay back on his bed. "One thing I'm curious about."

"What's that?"

"Those two chicks. The ones you keep switchin' back and forth with. Which is numero uno?"

"None of your business." Don grinned to cover real embarrassment. "In other words I don't know."

"I dig that Kitty," said Beans. "She's got class."

"Sure, she has. Kitty's loaded with class."

"She turned down that Sanders cat for you."

"I've got news for you. She is now going out with Homer."

"You're puttin' me on!"

"Homer's going to be a vice-president in charge of things. My father says he's a very good man to be in charge."

"I believe your father. But marry him? Never!"

"He didn't ask you," said Don. "Hey, the hell with all of them. What about the game tonight?"

"They'll eat us alive," said Beans. "But the loser's end of the playoff is good enough for me."

"You think we can't beat them."

"I do."

"You really believe it?"

"Look at their record. Look at ours. No way, man."

Don said, "I know about the record. But we beat them once. Why can't we beat them four out of seven?"

"Because you and me, we ain't with it, not in their class."

"You say that? You, the great man?"

"Look, I'm a gunner, right? I get my share of the points. Maybe I'm a better floor man since Bud and coach have been on my back. But on defense—I don't shine, man. I ain't admittin' that to anybody but you. But it's true."

After a moment Don said, "What worries me is that you don't give a damn, do you?"

"I didn't. Not when I came to the Beavers."

"But you have tried."

"I've tried, man."

There was a tap at the door. Don went to it, admitted Coach Reed and Bud Alcorn. Beans jumped up from the bed.

Don said, "Hey, come in. We were just talking about our chances."

They sat down, Alcorn on the bed with his long legs extended, Reed in a chair. Beans went to a straight chair and straddled it, his face serious.

Hobie Reed said, "That's why we're here. To talk about our chances."

"We beat them once," said Don rather weakly.

"But they're a better club," Reed said. He stared at Beans. "You agree with that, don't you, Jordan?"

"They're a better club," said Beans.

"Much better than the Banshees?"

"Well . . . the Banshees played them even because they've got that bench."

"In other words the Banshees made them play the Banshee game, which is run, run, run."

"Well . . . more or less." Beans shifted his weight. "Look, I know what you're going to say. If I'd run and defend better and pass off more we might could win."

"Don't you think that's true?"

"I'm doin' all I can do," Beans said.

"That's what I'm afraid of," said Reed gently. "I wanted to tell you. Peanuts is with us."

"Peanuts? That's impossible!" said Don.

"The man went all the way," Bud Alcorn said. "He's been working on the beach in the sand. In the gym. With the doc. He can run."

"A little," amended Reed. "He plays our game, Beans. Do you understand?"

"Oh, I get it." Beans was flushed to his collar line.

"We can't beat the Jaybirds with outside shooting. There's nothing new about this or anything else in basketball. You match up the opposition as best you can. On one leg Peanuts knows how to play our game."

"So why tell me?" But there was no bombast in the voice of the youngster.

"Thought you might get some eyes, man," Alcorn said.

"Eyes? I got the best eyes on this club."

"Eyes for the open man," Bud told him. "Legs to run, eyes to make the right play."

"I do the best I can," he repeated doggedly.

Don Brand saw no reason to speak. He felt the deepest sympathy for his roommate but it was true that the Jaybirds had to be fought in a certain manner. He only hoped that Beans would not go off the deep end. He thought he knew how much the game meant to the kid. He doubted that anyone else had ever penetrated deep enough to know as much.

Reed was saying, "Don will start. I'll be using you in spots, Beans."

"Okay. The money's the same."

"I like first money," Alcorn said.

"Sure, who don't?" Beans managed a laugh. "Try and get it without me in there gunnin' for us."

"Our problem is to prevent them from scoring," Reed said. "To play tight. To run."

"Okay, I heard you." Beans went to the closet and took out a jacket. "Thanks a heap. I'll see you at the game."

The door closed with a bang behind him. Alcorn and Reed looked at Don. He shrugged.

"You told him," he said. "He didn't like it."

"It's the only way." Reed looked old and weary. "Bud and I have talked and talked. We can't get to him. He won't rid himself of those bad habits."

"He scored twenty-eight points per game playing part-time," Don said.

"How many did he give up?" Alcorn shook his head. "Coach is right. We didn't have a game until coach gave us one. We had stars. Like myself. You got right into it. Why can't that flake?"

"I don't know," Don said honestly. "I really don't. He's got everything, the hands, the speed, agility. And I believe he tries. But he's a shooter. It's . . . it's like a physical handicap. He only sees the basket."

"And that won't do." Reed stood up. "We're laying a lot on you, Don. Peanuts can't go far. Carey—well, we'll use him because he also plays the game. But it'll be you under the gun."

"Do you think I'm ready?"

Alcorn answered. "Maybe not. But you're what we got, man."

Don tried to smile. "Well, I'm not about to run out. I'll be there at game time."

"Bring your roomie," said Alcorn. "A couple of us might get ourselves killed in there against Kane and company."

They left the room. Don sat and stared at the wall.

Kitty McCoy and Homer Sanders left the dinner table and followed their host into his study. Mr. Brand had arranged comfortable chairs in line, facing a new color television set which boasted the largest screen that could be purchased. He brought a decanter of brandy and large snifters and placed them within reach.

He said, "The experts say it is impossible for the Beavers to win either of the two games at Northwest City. I believe this is a fallible premise."

"We beat them up there one time," said Kitty. "Why not once more?"

"Don't be disappointed," Sanders said. "Don't get your hopes too high."

"It is always necessary to face facts," Mr. Brand agreed. "On the other hand, Junior has been playing great basketball. That young Jordan is the best shot maker in the league. Frankly, if I were the coach I would play them together as a team."

"I've wondered about that," said Kitty. "It seems so reasonable."

"One doesn't interfere," Mr. Brand said. "But I almost called Mr. Reed."

Sanders coughed. "Er—I've been following the team as you have, sir. It appears that they have a philosophy which does not allow for use of two young, green players at the same time. I mean, they have what they call a game plan."

"Of course. Junior explained all that to me. Their problem is that while it brought them this far the odds seem to be that the Jaybirds have the answer to their game. Ergo, I would alter my plans." Mr. Brand inhaled the bouquet of the brandy. "I'm no expert, of course, but in my time I have met a lot of opposition. Strategy is strategy in any contest."

"I agree," said Kitty. It was uncomfortable how many times she disagreed with Homer Sanders. Still, he was patient and kind and unflagging in his devotion to her. She sat uneasily awaiting the start of the game.

Martha Hall heard the little foreign car pull into her driveway and went out to greet her visitor. Alicia Aster extricated her ample figure from behind the wheel and came running up the steps out of breath.

"Oh I was so afraid of being late. I worked until six, wouldn't you know? Grabbed a bite to eat—has it started?"

"Not yet, darling," said Martha. She had liked Alicia upon their meeting. They had become friends during the long season when Don and Beans were away for so many weeks and neither girl had wanted to date other men.

They went into the Hall den and sat together on a comfortable couch and regarded the glowing tube. A glib announcer was making alibis in advance for the Beavers.

Alicia said, "The papers are awful, the way they say we can't possibly win. You believe that?"

"Well, we know the game. Pa and the boys are out looking with their gang and they don't think we can win. It doesn't look good for us."

"But Beansy is the best basket shooter in the world. He told me so himself," said Alicia in all seriousness.

"The Jaybirds don't let you shoot whenever you want," Martha said. It was no use trying to make it clear to Alicia. Beans and Don had tried and failed.

"I know that much." She smiled. "I guess I don't know anything, really. Baseball, football, basketball—I get them confused. All I know is, I hope Beansy wins."

"You're really in love with him, aren't you, darling?"

"You know? I really am." Alicia was solemn. "If you'd have told me I was going to fall for a man this year . . . well, I'd have sent you to a head shrinker."

"Your career, you mean?"

"They picked up my option," said Alicia. "I've got a chance to do a picture. You wouldn't believe, angel, you really wouldn't. Things are breaking my way. Old, dumb me."

"You're not all that dumb. You're a doll."

Alicia gave her a quick hug. "I know me. Or I thought I did until that hillbilly basketballer came along. Honest, Martha, he's the craziest. I mean, he's too much."

"Groovy?" Martha suggested.

"You know what I mean. You've got a case, too."

"A case?" Martha withdrew a pace in her mind. "Oh... Not really. It's all basketball with Don and me."

"On account of that Kitty woman, you mean."

"Kitty's a friend of mine."

"Some kind of friend."

"Anyway, she's going out with Homer Sanders again."

"You bet. To make Don jealous. Look, I may be unhip and all that. But I know what every girl should know." Alicia was, for her, emphatic. "Next to Beansy I like that Don the best. He's a good guy, a white hat."

"Oh, yes. He's a white hat." She did not want to discuss Don. She was not certain of her own feelings. "Look. They're going to introduce the players."

"I'll shut up," said Alicia. "Still and all. I know what I know." She patted Martha's hand.

They sat together and watched the action on the tube.

The Beaver squad huddled. There was the moment of silence, of hand-touching, of dedication. The chill went down Don Brand's spine. It was always there despite the rigors of the interminable pro basketball season. It would always be the challenge, the mystique of the game, of meeting the enemy surrounded by teammates; it could never become a chore.

Killer Kane had his starters about him, was pounding a fist into a palm, exhorting them. It was the same for him, Don knew. Rough, tough, mean and wily . . . he was all basketballer. However, his butterflies-in-the-tummy were unquestionably fitted with iron wings.

It was, after all, the world championship of basketball. It was a time for giving all that a man had and then reaching down and giving some more. It is not often that the chance for immortality in any endeavor is offered, Don Brand knew. To be a part of this team in his first year was the most he could desire in the world.

To him the prize in money was the least part. Since the first meeting with Hobie Reed in his father's office he had worked toward one goal, making the team. His life had been vastly altered by his own decision. The new life was what he had wanted and here was the culmination, against the Jaybirds and Killer Kane.

He saw Beans Jordan looking at him, trying to smile, clasping hands together in encouragement. He knew what it meant to Beans to be benched. His heart slowed the beat for a second or two. Beans also had a way of life. It had not fitted into the scheme of things but he could not think less of his roommate for this reason. He tried to convey sympathy to Beans without words, hoped that it was understood.

Bud Alcorn said, "We go, you dudes."

They went out as they were introduced. There was no politeness among the Jaybird rooters. They were booed and jeered. Northwest City was unaccustomed to bigtime sports. They lined up: Red Farber, Charlie Mount, Bud, Johnny Krash, and Don. They took their positions after the anthem was badly played over the loudspeaker system by a brass-band recording. Killer Kane was already on the prowl for him, Don was aware.

On the bench Hobie Reed sat amidst his reserves, bright-eyed, slightly flushed. He had talked to Dorothy and the boys on the telephone an hour ago. His future was riding on this series and they all knew it.

Peanuts Hopwood's knee was heavily bandaged but his spirit was as chirrupy as ever. He talked in a continuous monotone, reading the play, watching with bright eyes. Beside him was Beans Jordan listening, silenced for now. Farrell, Felton, Harper, Carey, all differences forgotten for the moment, were as tense and involved as the players on the court. The great starting moment was at hand.

Arnold, Heller, Drabski, Carr—they all had Kane's fire in their eyes. Their muscles gleamed as though oiled. They were rough and tough and scarred and proud. They were the Jaybirds, hailed by all as coming champions.

The official held the round ball in his hands. The din of the mob subsided. There was one fleeting moment of silence.

The whistle blew. The ball ascended toward the ceiling. Bud Alcorn uncoiled in his mighty leap. The game began.

The ball went to Farber—nobody outjumped Alcorn at any time. He dribbled to the left. Don went to his place, his pulse returned to normal with the sound of the ball tap-

tapping under the skilled direction of the great Beaver forward.

Kane applied himself to Krash, the forward and best jump-shot man. Don extricated himself from a jostling Cal Carr and went into the lane.

Farber gave it to Alcorn who faked for the basket, then laid it off to Don, who took it and went high, shooting. Without looking, he knew it was going through. When his feet hit the floor he was already racing down the court to take his place in the defense with the other Beavers. Scoring the first two points meant nothing—it was the final two that would make or break the evening.

Kane had the ball. Don went after him. Kane made one of his remarkable, crablike moves. Don tried to stay close. Kane passed off to Arnold. Don started to cover. An elbow smacked across the bridge of his nose.

He went down hard. Stars exploded and ran their course and vanished. Tears streamed down his cheeks. He was dazed. He tried to get up, fell back, bewildered as much as hurt. Whistles were blowing; a foul was being awarded. He put a hand to his face.

Hobie Reed was bellowing at the officials that Kane should be expelled from the game. Bud Alcorn picked up Don and carried him to the bench. A doctor bustled over with his black bag. Peanuts, his good nature gone, took off his sweat jacket and significantly spat on his hands, staring at Beans Jordan.

"Man," he said, "it's you and me, now. And do we carry it to that son?"

Beans said, "You start on him, Peanuts."

The doctor's hands were quick and sure. "Broken," he said. "I'll take him to the hospital and attend to it at once."

Don found he could speak. "And bring me back here."

"Of course," said the doctor.

Peanuts went onto the court. They led Don from the arena. The game continued with Killer Kane still on the field of action.

The doctor's name was Axelman. He turned on the car radio to the local sports broadcast and drove toward the hospital, only a few moments away. The towel which Don held to his face was red with blood.

The sportscaster said, "Hopwood is noticeably slower than before he was injured . . . now the Jaybirds have the ball. Kane brings it downcourt with terrific speed. Hopwood cannot cover . . . Kane scores over him . . . twelve to six for the Jaybirds. Their attack is tremendous . . . Krash bringing it across center court for the Beavers . . . He passes to Alcorn on the low post . . . Alcorn to Farber . . . To Mount . . . To Alcorn again, the Jaybirds are falling back on the post, Alcorn gives to Krash . . . Krash shoots . . . he misses! Drabski has the rebound . . ."

Dr. Axelman said, "They don't do as well without you, do they?"

Don mumbled an answer. His eyes were swollen. This worried him more than the aching nose.

When they came to the hospital the Jaybirds were leading the Beavers eighteen to twelve.

The emergency room was white and bright and bleak. A pert young nurse named Callahan was waiting. They put Don down on a table. Dr. Axelman had cool, efficient hands. There was a blinding flash of pain, then the nurse inserted a needle in his arm and Don voiced complaint.

"Hey! I've got to get back inna game." His voice was still not right.

"Don't be a fool, man," said Dr. Axelman. "Heroics are for schoolboys."

The pain lessened. Nurse Callahan wiped out his eyes. The flesh around them was swollen. His vision was distorted. Don sat up.

"I'b a schoolboy," he said. "Gotta get back."

Dr. Axelman said, "You could hemorrhage, you know. Another blow—exertion—many things could cause it."

A severe lady came with papers. "This man wasn't signed in, Dr. Axelman. You know the rules."

Don said, "Gibbe the papers. Just so I get ouda here."

He scribbled his name. Dr. Axelman shrugged and said, "Well, I'm a fan. Let's go, then."

They drove back to the auditorium. The announcer said, "As the half draws to an end it is plain the Jaybirds are in charge . . . time out now . . . Beans Jordan is being put into the game for the first time . . . he's the gunner . . . We know Beans, he was with the Jaybirds . . . not a team man . . . the Beavers are desperate for points, trailing forty-eight to thirty-eight with time running out . . ."

"Interesting case, Jordan," observed the doctor. "I wonder what is really the matter with him."

"Nod a hell of a lod," said Don. He touched the plaster which covered the splints on his nose.

The announcer said, "Jordan has the ball thirty feet out . . . he shoots! He makes it! A remarkable offhand shot which he can make once in a blue moon . . . Kane is bringing the ball back . . . Jordan is faster getting down on defense than when he was here . . . Jordan steals the ball from Kane! The first turnover by the brilliant Jaybird guard . . . Alcorn takes the pass . . . to Mount . . . Mount moves in . . . jumps . . . dunks! Four quick points for the Beavers makes it forty-eight to forty-two for the home team . . ."

"Go, Beans, go," muttered Don. "Show 'em."

"Flashy but not steady," pronounced the doctor.

"Duts," said Don. His "n" was difficult to pronounce. A head cold would have been a pleasure. The injection was wearing off—maybe the nurse was a Jaybird fan —and the pain was there like a toothache in his nose.

The announcer's voice rose to a yell, "Jordan's going crazy . . . He just stole it again from Kane . . . Killer's after him now . . . Jordan drives for the basket with Kane on him . . . Jordan shoots . . . no . . . no . . . he faked it . . . he passes to Krash . . . Johnny scores! Kane is furious . . he collides with Jordan . . . Kane goes down! Players rush at each other . . . the benches are empty, folks . . . there's a fight going on . . . the officials are trying to stop it . . . oh, Bud Alcorn picked up Kane and threw him off the floor . . . threw him! Cooler heads are prevailing . . . Kane runs back on the court but his own men surround him . . . The score is now forty-eight to forty-four, thanks to brilliant play by Beans Jordan . . . face it, folks, it's a new Beans on the court tonight . . ."

"See what I bean?" Don said to the doctor. They parked and ran into the big hall.

Hobie Reed knelt in front of the Beaver bench, pounding his fist on the floor, silent, but taut as a violin string. The other players were all leaning and shouting. No one noticed Don when he came and perched at the end of the line of men, his warm-up jacket stained with his blood.

Killer Kane was going after Beans. The clock was running down. Beans was laughing and making moves like a ballet dancer. The ball got away from a Jaybird and Jordan had it. He slung it to Charlie Mount, who gave it to Farber, who passed long down the court to Krash. Drabski loomed over Krash on a mismatch switch. Johnny bounce-passed.

Beans was there. He went up and up. He dunked the ball. It became forty-eight to forty-six. The horn ended the first half of play.

The Jaybird fans were stunned to silence. Hobie Reed beamed like a lighthouse on a dark night. He spotted Don.

"Did you see it? Did you see Beans go?" Then he said, "Oh, Don. How is it? Are you all right?"

"Doe, I'b dot awright," said Don. "But I cad play."

"You won't have to play." Reed put his arm around Don and they walked together to the dressing room. Catcalls and jeers came half-heartedly from the fans in tiers above them. They closed the door and shut out the sounds.

Beans was at Don's side. "Does it hurt? I laid one on him, roomie. I really put it to him, man."

Bud asked wonderingly, "Whatever got into you, Beansy-boy? You were too much!"

"The dirty rat bombed my roomie, didn't he? Got away with it, didn't he? You know he did it on purpose."

"You know it and I know it—but the officials don't want to know it," said Hobie Reed. "It boomeranged, didn't it?"

It was odd but Beans wasn't emotional about it, Don thought. He was apparently his usual beaming self. Only his hands betrayed him—they shook a little as he wiped away the sweat and sat on the bench.

"Ad' the way t' go," Don said to him.

"You talk funny," said Beans.

"Uh-huh."

"Peanuts can't cut it," Beans whispered. "The guts of two bears but his knee won't stand it. Farrell's too slow. Sure hope Hobie sees it."

"Hobie sees all." The words came easier all at once. His nasal passages were draining. "I can play."

"You stay on the bench until I fall over," Beans said. "Hobie won't keep me out now, I don't think. I'm hot and when you're hot, man, you're hot."

The trainer and the coach were counting bruises inflicted by the rough Jaybirds. There were too many. Drabski had managed to kick Bud on the bad knee. Krash had a nicked ear. Mount's left arm was swollen from elbow jabs. Farber sported an incipient black eye. Peanuts was hobbling.

"They got some knocks, too," said Bud.

"Loved seein' you take out Kane," said Beans. "It was beautiful, man."

"I had a notion to turn him on his head," said the big center. "Knew it wouldn't do us any good, though."

"Two lousy points," said Mount. "Nothin', dudes. Just let's keep on top of 'em."

Don had never seen Bud's cousin so worked up. The entire team seemed to be afire. Each player came by to touch him, nod to him, wink at him. Peanuts put an arm around him and spoke in his ear.

"Did my best, brother. But Beansy-boy is terrific. He's higher than a kite. Maybe Carey and me can work spots for him this half. Just so he stays wound up."

Don nodded. "That's the whole barrel."

"They were talkin'—he's your buddy, all that. Now they can see what it means to have a buddy."

Peanuts was right, Don knew. Something had to touch Beans down deep to bring him to action. It was touching to know that his own injury had sparked the wild kid from the hills. It was almost worth a busted nose . . . almost but not quite.

Reed said, "Beans, can you keep it up?"

"I'm wild tonight," said Jordan.

"You start. We'll substitute a bit more this half to give you veterans some rest. So—while you're in there show them you're the best starting five in the business."

He said no more. Time was called and they went out to the court. Don took his turn with the others in the warm-up. At first he couldn't focus on the basket. Gradually his eyes cleared and he began to drop the ball through the net. He found that he was not weakened in any way. He ran to midcourt. He found himself returning the stare of Killer Kane.

He said softly, "Try me again, sucker."

"You better believe it," snapped Kane.

"Better look out. Bud'll getcha," mocked Don. He turned away laughing before Kane could answer. He could imagine the humiliation suffered by the fighting Kane when Alcorn handled him like a sack of potatoes.

Hobie Reed called them to the bench. He said, "Try and give Beans a sideline. Okay?"

"Right on," said Bud Alcorn.

Don sat down. The officials split, each to a bench, the third man standing in midcourt with the ball.

"This is a warning," said the referee to the Beavers. "We're going to crack down on roughness. No more fights, understand?"

"Just so the Killer understands," said Hobie Reed sharply.

"He'll understand. He's getting the same message. The commissioner called between halves. He's hot."

"We're a bit on the warm side. Look at Brand."

"Okay. Just watch it."

Beans grinned at Don. "Let them watch it, roomie."

The teams went to their positions. Killer Kane began wandering in his catlike way. The ball went up. Bud got the jump and tapped to Farber. Kane tried to steal the ball. Farber gave him the hip and spun, dribbling. Beans was down the left sideline. The Beavers formed a picket line.

Farber passed high. Beans jumped and took it and strode on. The defense tried to get to him. Beans braked. He jumped and shot from twenty feet.

The ball went through the iron and the score was tied. Now the stands were yelling to their team to "do something, you jerks." It was certainly a bush-league crowd, Don thought. Kane was bringing the ball downcourt with all his skill and speed. He evaded two men and faced Beans. He gave a head fake, then a shoulder fake.

Beans stayed with him. Kane passed off and bumped Beans. A whistle blew.

Beans made his foul shots. The Beavers were ahead for the first time since the opening minute. The referee was shaking a finger at Kane, who smouldered but refused to give reason to be thrown out of the game.

If the Jaybirds could be restrained the odds were leveled, Don thought. Hobie Reed had taught the virtue of the fundamentals of basketball to his men. The game went on, fast and furious. The Jaybirds began to score as Kane brought down the ball and Arnold got loose for his sure shots.

And Beans continued to use the black lines where the defenders could only attack him from one side. Not once did he go skylarking helter-skelter in his former fashion. When they blocked him he took the long shot. Once he missed but Charlie Mount went a mile into space to grab the rebound and stuff it for two points.

The pace was too much for human lungs. The Jaybird coach finally made changes in the lineup.

Hobie Reed said at once, "Farrell for Alcorn. Harper for Mount. Felton for Krash. Carey for Farber." He hesitated. "Hopwood for Jordan."

Peanuts shook his head. "I'm sorry all to pieces, Hobie. My knee's stiffened up. I can't bend it."

Don was on his feet. Reed looked doubtful. Don took off his sweat suit. Reed didn't like it but Jordan was certainly needful of a rest.

"Just a couple of minutes, Don," the coach finally agreed.

Don took the court. There was a murmur in the crowded stands. Then a few Jaybird fans began to applaud. Northwest City was growing up to pro basketball—it gave Don a warm feeling.

Kane gave him the usual glare. It was Beavers toss-in on the time out called by the Jaybirds. Don took the ball. Kane danced in front of him, arms waving. The score was now Beavers seventy-four, Jaybirds sixty-eight.

Beans yelled, "Put it it to 'em, roomie."

Don faked, then reversed his direction and fed Carey, the steady if not sensational sub guard. Carey went down the court against the Jaybird second string, only Kane remaining of their starters. Kane checked in, rapping at the ball. Don went past him. Alcorn screened off Kane when he tried to switch. Carey passed to Don.

The jump shot was from fifteen feet without opposition. The ball went in and the score rose to Beavers seventy-six, Jaybirds sixty-eight. Beans was hollering his head off from the bench.

Don wished Beans would save his breath. He was quickly aware that breathing through the mouth was unnatural to him. He ran and ran but he was tiring fast.

He came face to face with Kane as the Jaybird guard was driving for the basket. He threw up his arms, giving the required distance but staying between Killer and the basket. He saw the hatred in the man's eyes. He swerved his head to one side.

Kane was butting toward his face. Don bent low. Kane could not stop his charge. The foul was called at once by the referee. Don made his foul shots.

Hobie Reed called for the time out. Beans was on his feet laughing like a loon.

"Faked him into the rafters," Beans chortled. "Lemme at him, pal. My turn."

Reed said, "Sit down, Don. It was beautiful."

The Beavers of the first string all returned to the field of play. Jaybirds came to match up. The game went on.

Now the pace was slowed. The Jaybirds were afraid of committing fouls. Kane was in trouble with four against him. Drabski had three. None had less than two.

And Hobie Reed's game plan took effect. When the Jaybirds could not go man for man at a furious pace they were not as cohesive, they lacked confidence. Only Killer Kane moved like a whirling dervish about the floor to keep the score close.

The man was better when he was not indulging in roughness, Don thought, watching closely every move made by the great guard of the Jaybirds. There was a connection between Kane and Beans Jordan in a way—

each had trouble not in his athletic abilities but in his head.

Time, as always, was running out. The Beavers led, eighty-six to eighty-one. Kane was deft and swift. Mount missed a shot and Drabski took the rebound and passed off. Kane went around the defenders like a cooper around a barrel. He scored. He was playing wildly but brilliantly, taking all responsibility upon himself as his teammates floundered under the full-court press of the Beavers.

Suddenly, as Kane was dribbling furiously after another bad shot by Mount, Beans Jordan seemed to come alive again. He darted in. His hand was a blur of brown action as he snatched away the ball. The tanned, blond young man whirled and looked for an open man. He sailed a high one to Bud. He ran down the sideline. He evaded Kane in the corner, took the return pass and scored with the nonchalance which was as much a part of him as his floppy hair.

The horn blew for an ending. Kane stood like a statue for a moment, directing his glare first at Beans, then at Don on the bench. Then he ran for the dressing room at top speed, unable to face the disappointed fans and his own outrage at defeat.

The celebration was mild. The Beavers were hurting all over. Don's head ached. He took aspirin and still it ached. He went back to the hotel room with Beans and asked that his after-game supper be sent up to him.

Beans was solicitous. He was also dressed to go out.

"Well, when I was mopin' there, you know, when Hobie got on me? Well, I met a girl, see? Real nice girl. Promised to have supper with her. You just try to get some sleep, roomie. I'll be in early."

Don shook his head then stopped because it hurt. "No way to stop you and the dames."

"It's just for company—relaxin', you know?"

"Sure, I know. You bet I know."

He ought to call his father, he thought. His brow was hot. His nose hurt and there were bruises on his arms and legs from the heavy contact during the game. He lay down. It was impossible to get comfortable. Each way he turned seemed to hurt his face.

He slept fitfully, dreaming. Finally he awakened and knew he was burning with fever. It was two o'clock in the morning. The door to the room opened and Beans tiptoed in.

Don said thickly, "I think I'm sick."

Beans put a hand on his forehead. He said, "You're sick all right, roomie."

The next thing Don remembered clearly was Dr. Axelman and Nurse Callahan at the side of a bed which was not in the hotel. He recognized the inevitable white walls and stark lights. He was back in the hospital. He scarcely felt the prick of the needle as it went into his vein.

Then it was morning. Someone was at his bedside. He blinked and said, "Hey, father. How'd you get here?"

"The company jet," said Mr. Brand. "When you didn't call we made inquiries."

"It's just a busted nose," said Don with difficulty.

"It may well have been pneumonia," said his father. "It isn't. A reaction, Dr. Axelman said. If you feel able we can fly home to Dr. Boardman."

"I kind of like Dr. Axelman," said Don. His eyes were heavy. "Awful nice of you to fly up."

"You *are* my son."

"Lucky . . . to have . . . a father like you." He simply could not remain awake.

He slept through the day. The game over television was a haze to him. Killer Kane had somehow pulled his team together overnight. The Beavers without either Peanuts or Don were below par. They fought hard, they met every challenge as bravely as possible. But the Jaybirds evened the series, 102 to 98.

Don felt the blow but he soon was again asleep. The series would now go to Canyon City with a day off before the third meeting of the two clubs. Mr. Brand retained the jet. The team went home—Don remained in the care of Nurse Callahan. It wasn't until the day of the resumption of play that he flew in with his father and was driven to Grove Estates where Dr. Boardman pronounced him fit—except for the slowly healing broken nose.

"Undoubtedly sheer exhaustion plus the reaction of the injury," said the eminent physician.

"I want a face guard," Don said. "There's a special kind."

His father hesitated. Then he said, "Yes. I knew you would. One will be delivered today."

9

When the white, ghostly mask arrived at Grove Estates Martha Hall, Alicia Aster, and Beans Jordan were lounging beside the Brand pool with Don. The girls squealed in pretended fear when Don tried it on.

Beans said, "Won't scare the Killer none, roomie."

"Nothing scares the Killer." The mask felt strange and he still had to breathe through his mouth. "This'll take getting used to."

"It doesn't do a thing for your manly beauty," said Martha.

"How did you get off work?" asked Don.

"Oh, didn't I tell you? I quit," she said, not looking at him. "Pa decided I shouldn't work any longer."

"I thought you liked it at the company."

"I did." She offered no further comment.

Beans said, "Smart kid. Why work? Hey, it's hot. Let's get wet."

The sun shone on their glistening bodies as Alicia and Beans jumped into the pool. Don took off the mask.

"You had trouble at the company," he said to Martha.

"Not trouble. Not really."

"Kitty?"

She frowned. "Not altogether. But . . . well, since Homer Sanders took over and Kitty sort of became his aide . . . It wasn't the same. They're . . . very efficient. They hired a Phi Beta Kappa from UCLA to take my place."

"As receptionist?"

"With a future, they told her. She wears thick glasses and midi-skirts."

"Am I glad I'm out of there!" He grinned at her. "You

know I could write a song. 'Your Bikini Becomes You.' "

"How nice of you to notice." But she flushed behind the flippancy of her retort.

They ate together. Mr. Brand joined them halfway through the meal served by the cook. They talked basketball. It was not surprising to Don that his father now knew as much about the science of the game as a layman could possibly learn.

Beans was fascinated. "Hey, man . . . I mean, sir. I thought you didn't dig the game?"

"You were correct," said Mr. Brand. "I have learned that when Dr. Naismith hung a peach basket on the wall he invented a game that is second only to softball in the number of people indulging in it."

"No kiddin'?"

"The playgrounds of America breed basketball stars," said Mr. Brand. "The professionals have advanced it to what is more appropriately a ballet than a science. Unlike football, similar to baseball, nothing new has been added for years. The skill and courage of the individuals in the pro ranks decided the issue."

"You know what?" Beans beamed. "He's right!"

Don had never seen his father quite so proud. Martha winked across the table.

Alicia said, "I think it's cute, the way Mr. B has taken up the game. I still don't know up from down about it."

"I have had the advantage of speaking with Pat Hall," said Mr. Brand. "Thanks to Martha's intervention." He peered at Martha. "I still don't quite understand why you left us, my dear. It's not the same without your smiling countenance."

"Pa thought I'd better keep house. Our lady left us and it was getting tacky around the place."

"Too bad," said Mr. Brand. "I must say the new girl has taken hold. Kitty approves of her."

"That's wonderful," said Martha demurely. Again she met Don's eyes with a small smile.

Don said, "Only two and a half hours to game time. We'd better get cookin'."

His father nodded. "I wish you wouldn't try to play. But I know you must if you think it right."

"You'll be there?"

"Of course." Mr. Brand smiled. "I've become an addict."

They got into the Maserati and Beans drove with his usual flourish to the Canyon City arena. The girls took the car for an errand of their own and the men went into the dressing room. They were not the first to arrive, for Coach Reed and Bud Alcorn were seated together, talking.

Beans said, "I hope you cats have got something figured to slow down that Killer."

"He's phenomenal," said Reed. "Fully recovered from his surgery and smarter than ever." He touched the mask in Don's hand. "Once talked to you about drive, dedication. Didn't mean for you to commit hari-kari, you know."

"I've had a day's rest. I'm fine."

"I shouldn't have let you play up north," said Reed.

"I'll be fine for spots when you need me."

"You can suit up," said Reed. "And watch."

Don went to his locker. He had not expected this opposition. Charlie Mount came in, fingered the white mask.

"Should've got a black one," he said, grinning. "The Jaybird soul brothers wouldn't know you."

"Your soul brothers, not mine," retorted Don. "They hurt you, those brothers."

"They ain't kiddin' around. But hey, man that roomie of yours has got what it takes."

"He means well." Don knew Mount and some others had disliked and distrusted Beans from the first.

"Hey, well . . . you, too," said Mount.

"Thanks," said Don. "All the brothers are valiant."

"I dig," said Mount delightedly. "Had it in college. From an epitaph on a tombstone in . . . where?"

"Westminster Abbey," said Don. "It's 'were' valiant, not 'are' valiant."

"Hey man, what about that? Duchess of . . . of Newcastle." Mount was hugely pleased. "All the brothers were valiant. Hey, man, that's us."

A mutual quondam memory had forged a small but useful bond, Don thought, changing into his uniform. The overlong season had naturally created tensions, now they were evaporating. Now if they could put it all together they might win. He was suddenly aware that down deep he had never truly believed the Beavers could beat the Jaybirds. He had thought that he was too green, that Beans was too wild and the veterans too aged.

The trainer came and gave him a package. He unwrapped it. There was a note, "Maybe this will help the breathing . . . Martha."

It was a small oxygen cylinder with a mouthpiece. He tried it and his lungs expanded and seemed to work more normally. He looked at the note again. It began, "Love . . ."

Love, he thought. Songs ran through his head. Love of Martha Hall who was always warm and always thoughtful. They were the best of friends, of course. . . .

And what of Kitty McCoy?

A friend of Homer's, he answered himself. Friends . . .

Hobie Reed was taking them out for the preliminary warm-ups. He put everything else aside in another corner of his mind and went out to renew his acquaintance with the home-site boards.

The gates opened and the fans came in, first the general admissions filling the top rows, then the season-ticket holders. He saw the Halls and then his father came with Kitty and Homer and took their choice seats. He had time for a word with them.

Kitty said, "You're not going to play!"

"Who knows?"

Homer said, "Good show, Junior. Good show."

His father said, "Don't get hurt again, son. Please."

He looked at his father. He said, "I'll do my best, sir."

It was enough. They were close together now—he understood the concern, he heard it in the voice of his father. He had broken the shell and gone like a chick into the world and his life had become his own and his father approved, he knew. His father was thinking it through, arriving at the conclusion best for the son. Now he must have concern for the father.

They went to the dressing room for a last-moment confab, then to rest, then back out to the court. Don carried his little oxygen tank. The team had its own supply but he felt better using this at his private convenience. He sat on the bench through the formalities of opening the championship series in Canyon City. Individual play, his father had said, but it was more than that. It was keying off the play of each individual, friend and foe. It was timing and the best possible use of mind and body.

Beans started at guard. Peanuts sat alongside Don and talked in his easy manner.

"I got maybe a couple minutes. You shouldn't go in tonight, man. No way. They won't need you that bad. First game here, you watch our guys."

It was true. From the first tip, Alcorn to Farber, the Beavers ran like stallions in the wilds. At the half the score was Beavers fifty-nine, Jaybirds forty-five. There was no need for Don. Beans scored twenty points. Peanuts relieved him and dazzled even Kane with his footwork for the brief spells he was in there.

Late in the second half with the score still in favor of the Beavers Killer Kane started another rally. Beans was tiring. Reed put in Ed Carey. Kane ran around Carey and scored twice.

Don said, "Please, Hobie."

The coach said reluctantly, "Two minutes, that's all."

Don put on the mask. The crowd stood and roared for the game hometown boy. If nothing else it was good public relations, thought Don. He saw Kane's look of disgust. He laughed behind the mask. Kane could not attack him now, and the Jaybirds had to go all out on offense.

So he carried it to Kane. He went after the ball. He caught the elbow but turned his head and took it on the muscles of his back. He harassed Kane so that Farber came in and blocked the ball to Krash.

Alcorn was going in. Krash gave him the pass. Bud went up and stuffed. When he came down he slipped. He hit the floor with a resounding crash.

Farrell came hustling in. The game ran out with the Jaybirds scoring but not catching up. The Beavers won, 116 to 104.

But Bud Alcorn's knee was swollen again. It seemed that the fates would not allow the Beavers to quite "get it all together." The trainer shook his head. They brought in the doctor and did what they could but it looked bad, Don knew.

"Complete rest for at least two days," the doctor said. "I'll take an x-ray tomorrow."

George Farrell was pale around the gills. He had to replace one of the all-time greats on national television in a crucial championship game. He had to go with very little relief. Don felt the greatest sympathy for the big man.

His father and Kitty and Martha and Homer were awaiting him. He went out with Beans. They drove to a nearby restaurant for a snack. He could not rationalize, and he was disheartened. Martha understood. Kitty railed at him, Homer tried to make jokes but Beans was also quiet, subdued. It was not a cheery evening for the Beaver cohorts.

"You'd think we lost," Beans said mournfully.

"We did," said Don. "We lost our big man."

"Amen."

They left the place. On the way home Don spoke to Martha aside from the others.

"Thanks for the oxygen. It was good to have it."

"You're welcome." She sighed. "You can't win without Bud, can you?"

"No. We may win a game but not a series."

"What about the next game?"

"I don't know. Farrell—well, it's a lot to ask."

She said, "I'm so sorry."

"Don't be." He held her hand. "The world will go on, and people will live and breathe. We've got a great team. Great men. We're pros—we'll survive."

"You're proud of being a pro, aren't you, Don?"

"It's what I wanted. I wish I were better at it."

She snuggled closer to him. "You're good enough. You're plenty good enough."

Kitty had never said anything close to that to him. Kitty and Homer seemed right together now, somehow or other. He kissed Martha good night for the first time.

It was a good, close feeling they had between them. He drove home with Beans and watched the blond youth head for his singles with Alicia by his side. If it were not for his busted nose and Bud's knee the world would look mighty fine, he thought.

At game time the stands were buzzing, the broadcaster was moaning, the Jaybirds were cocky and confident. Don inhaled his oxygen, found he could breathe better now. It had been decided by the medicos that Bud Alcorn should not suit up, that he should have complete rest for his knee. The big center and captain was still at the hospital.

Beans was to start at guard. In the huddle before the opening whistle Don suddenly spoke up.

"It's not a funeral, you cats! Give George some help. Let's carry it to 'em."

Reed added quickly, "That's the story. Get on 'em. Make 'em believe it."

Nothing new, Don thought. Nothing in the world novel about psyching up the ballplayers. But he saw Beans sparkle a little and he saw Krash and Farber, the quiet men, compress their lips and he saw Charlie Mount flex his muscles. Then they were on the court to face the Killer and his crew.

The ball took its trip upward. George Farrell jumped with all his strength. Drabski went above him and tapped to Kane. The Jaybirds rolled down the floor like a swollen river and scored two points.

Farber brought it back. Beans took the right sideline. Kane got over to break up the design of the play. Beans took a pass right off Kane's nose and turned and shot still another long one.

It dropped in and the score was tied at two all.

Kane took it back but now the Beavers were all over him, all over every Jaybird. Farrell interfered with Drabski's notions of the play. Farber and Beans picked away at the ball. Arnold was forced to take a bad shot. Farrell went up and bullied the rebound away from Drabski.

Peanuts slapped Don's knee. "You see that, man? George has got his dauber up."

Farber had the ball. He dribbled with Kane on him, came to the sagging defense of the Jaybirds, stopped in his tracks. Farrell was slow coming down. Beans was covered like a tent. Farber passed to Krash and cut for the basket. Since he was not known as a scoring threat he was not covered. Krash bounced to him below Kane's waving arms.

Farber put the ball into the basket to make it four to two, the Beavers. The crowd reacted, cheering the heroes, Farrell and Johnny Krash.

"They got it," Peanuts gloated. "They got the fever."

Overlooked athletes became cool professionals doing their thing. The Jaybirds, geared to face Bud Alcorn, were slightly confused. Farrell performed feats of daring and courage and Farber got loose again. Beans Jordan was into it, stealing the ball or causing turnovers by his persistent defense. Krash had the eye for the hoop as always and Beans got the ball to him. At the half the rebuilt, handicapped Beavers led fifty to thirty-eight.

In the dressing room the atmosphere was subtly different. There was more exaltation than exultation. Hobie Reed spoke quietly to Don.

"This is unreal. I don't trust this feeling. It's a bubble that can be punctured. It's not professional."

"Maybe. Maybe it is a bit schoolboy," said Don. "But it's working."

"I may have to use you. Beans is going too hard," said the coach, looking at the blond youth.

Beans had his head in a cold towel. One leg moved back and forth, the calf muscles twitching.

"I can play," said Don. He went over and sat beside Beans and asked, "How you doing, roomie?"

"How 'bout that Farrell?" Beansy's voice was high, shrill. "How 'bout that Farber and Krash?"

"You're all beautiful," said Don.

"You better believe it."

But Hobie was right, Don thought. Beans was playing on his nerve right now. He was working automatically, doing the things he had not done before. It was going against his nature and it could not last.

The second half began. Beans took a pass and looked for someone to whom to pass off. Killer Kane came in hard. He slapped away the ball before Beans could detect his purpose. The Jaybirds scored to make it fifty to forty for the home team.

"Next time out," the coach said to Don. "You sure you can do it?"

"I can give him a rest while you talk to him."

It was teamwork and it was a delicate thing. Beans was overdoing it. The Jaybirds called for the time and Don took off his jacket. Beans looked a bit blurry as he came off. The Jaybirds had scored again to cut the lead to eight points, never secure in the high scoring pro game.

The mask allowed for peripheral vision. Don put the ball into play to Farber. Kane was there at once, hanging onto Don's flank, suspecting a stratagem. Farber got the ball to Farrell on the post. Drabski went in to challenge Farrell. The ball came to Don.

Kane came in close, eyes fierce as always. Don turned his back, bent low, dribbling. Krash broke loose. Don moved as though to pass off. Kane switched with that catlike quickness.

Don held the ball. He spun around and shot without hindrance. He scored two points.

Kane had the ball. Farrell and Drabski clashed and the Jaybird was the aggressor and there was a foul. The big sub center took his shot with cool calmness and made it good.

It was no miracle, Don thought, trying to breathe properly behind the mask. It was constant practice, careful watching of the opponents, good execution. Farrell was playing over his former skills but he was meeting a challenge and doing it superbly.

Again the Jaybirds took time out, disbelieving that the Beavers could play so well without Alcorn. At the bench Hobie looked at him and nodded, then said, "Peanuts will try it."

"All right with me," said Don. He was breathing in gasps. He sat down alongside of Beans.

"Hey, great," said Beans. The fuzzy look had evaporated, he was himself again. "Hobie says I was going far out. Guess I was, at that. Farrell, he got me steamed, playin' as good as he is."

"But can he go all the way? He's been on the bench a lot," said Don.

"Coach has got a notion," said Beans. "Hold everything."

Farrell managed well until the last five minutes. Don could see him begin to wilt under the strain, the continual running demanded by Reed's game plan. There was a time out and the team came to the bench.

Reed said, "Okay, George. Charlie, how about playing center?"

Mount looked startled, then he grinned. "Right on, coach."

"All right, then Jordan and Brand go at guard, Krash and Farber up front. Okay?"

Farber was not certain. "Who quarterbacks?"

"You do," Reed told him. "Just play the game like always."

"Oh. I see." The designations meant nothing. The idea was to get five men playing together on the floor and let the Jaybirds worry about match-ups. Charlie Mount wasn't nearly as tall as Moe Drabski but he was as strong as an ox. The team went back on the court.

Again it seemed that the man-for-man play of the Jaybirds was distracted by the new lineup. Kane could not get loose. The Beavers scored twice.

Kane went after Don. Twice he committed roughness fouls, both times Don stepped away from him and converted his free throws.

Kane growled, "I'll rip that mask off you before you're through, chicken-boy."

"Why don't you?" Don taunted him. "Hard to see you, grandma."

"I'll grandma you!"

The referee said, "That's enough, Kane!"

The star Jaybird guard did everything but froth at the mouth. He also began to play like a madman. The score became closer as he got the ball to Arnold several times. Don had trouble with his breathing but he was able to play his position. It seemed odd to be on the court with Beans and this threw him off a bit, but they began to get the feel of each other's play as time ran out.

Kane was making a last run at it with the Jaybirds 10

points behind at 114 to 104. Don drifted in and drove him away from the sideline. Beans closed with him.

The ball came loose. Don snatched it up. Beans was already flying downcourt. Don straightened. He reached back and threw the ball with all his might.

Beans rose like a leaping swordfish and plucked the ball from the air. He shot before his feet touched the boards. The net fluttered as the leather dropped through. It was a perfect instinctive play by the two guards of the Beavers.

The game ended. The Beavers had achieved the impossible. They would go back to Northwest City holding a three-to-one lead in a four-of-seven series.

If they were not underdogs, if they were not injured and suffering, they would be prohibitive favorites to win. Farrell could not be expected to continue his brilliant play—the Jaybirds on their home court would be prepared for him and Drabski had the size to accomplish his downfall. The Beavers could not go with Mount at center. They needed Bud Alcorn, who was in the hospital.

All this went through Don's head in the locker room when he heard Reed calling for attention. The coach said, "A little surprise for you. Before the game Mr. Brand invited us all to the Now Then dining room for a supper. Wives, children, any of you who can attend. He's taken the place over for the evening."

Beans said, "How about that? Champagne, too, coach?"

"He'll be expecting everybody," Reed said.

Charlie Mount said, "I always knew there was a reason we hired that rich kid."

Don flushed but it was not as before—all was now good-natured wordplay. Spirit ran high as they dressed and hurried to tell their wives and girl friends the plan and to drive out to the restaurant. Don drove his convertible with Martha at his side. Her father and brothers were also invited, he learned.

She said, "Your father has really got with it, hasn't he?"

"I'm proud of him," said Don.

"He doesn't realize what goes, does he?"

"I don't know. He has that logical mind. Wouldn't surprise me if he guessed."

"If Bud can't play and Peanuts doesn't improve . . . you're in trouble up north."

"We're in trouble."

"It'll go seven games."

"You know it."

"How about you?"

"I can play if Kane doesn't get to my nose again."

"I think you'd better win one up there," she said. "What do you think?"

"I agree." He grinned at her. "How about flying up for the games?"

"Do you mean it?"

"It would help to have you there."

"Because I'm one of the Hall family?"

"Because you're you," he told her.

"Oh," she said. Then she added, "In that case—I'll be there."

They went on to the Now Then. Cars were arriving and they lingered, greeting their friends. When they went inside it was crowded and Don lost Martha in the crush as he sought his father.

Mr. Brand asked, "Have you seen Kitty? She was supposed to help. Hostess, you know?"

"Haven't laid eyes on her." He felt exhilarated and it was not the basketball victory, he knew, which made him elated. It was the fact that Martha was going to Northwest City.

At that moment Kitty entered. She was alone. Mr. Brand hurried to her, then brought her back to where Don stood against the wall with a glass of draft beer in his hand.

"Must rush," said Mr. Brand. "Must be sure to greet everyone."

Kitty took the beer and sipped at it. "You don't even like the stuff," she said.

"Where's Homer?"

She glanced at him sideways. "Gone home."

"Too many black folks?" he asked. "People not welcome at the country club?"

"I hate to admit it," she said. "He pled a headache and a busy tomorrow."

"Ugh," said Don.

"Ugh. . . . Ugh," she replied, nodding. "When are you going to ask me to go out with you, friend?"

He said, "Well. . . ." His tongue grew thick. He felt his cheeks burning.

She nodded again. "I blew it, didn't I?"

"Well. . . ."

"Little Martha. It's hard to believe. I shouldn't have fired her."

"I didn't know you had fired her."

"No, she wouldn't tell you that. She's too nice. But I did. Homer wanted more businesslike efficiency. The stern image of the science organization. She was too pretty and too sweet."

"She was happy to leave," Don told her.

"Was she? I'm glad." Kitty drained the beer. She said, "I must help your father. The basketball fan. My little world has turned topsy-turvy, Don . . . you're not Junior any more."

He felt sorry about it. For years he had believed she was his girl. For years he had dimly thought they might someday be married. True he had never thought about it in a concrete fashion—he had not visualized the details nor the future beyond the wedding.

It would have been a great error, he thought, going to join his teammates and their families.

10

Northwest City lay under sullen skies and rain poured down. Martha and Alicia Aster rode to the motel near the auditorium with Don, Beans, and Bud Alcorn.

"It's Jaybird weather," said Bud.

"They might think so," Beans said.

Bud was wearing a special leather-and-aluminum brace, they all knew. It was hinged at the knee and it would limit his playing time. Peanuts Hopwood had not improved.

Alicia said, "We finished shooting a day early so I could get off. Maybe that's good luck."

"We'll need it," said Bud. He was not in his usual confident mood, at least as to his own ability.

"Farrell was real good," Beans insisted. "If he keeps on playin' that way we'll be all right."

"I pray for him," said Bud.

They got out at the motel and went indoors. The girls had a room together on the second floor, apart from the players. Truthfully, Hobie Reed had not been enthusiastic about their presence, fearing distraction of his men. The coach was on edge for excellent reasons. Don unpacked his few belongings and sat down and looked at Beans.

"I'm going to play without that damn mask," he said. "I can breathe better. The adhesive is protection enough."

"Maybe. If you don't forget to duck."

"All right, I'll duck."

Beans said, "Everybody's on a bummer because of Bud's knee."

"Can you think of a better reason?"

"Tell you one thing, man. We're gonna lose tonight," Beans said. "You mind my words."

"I mind 'em."

They went to the hall. The rain did not prevent the fans from appearing in vast numbers. It was a hostile, uneasy crowd, aware that the Beavers needed but one game to sew up the championship.

The preliminaries were not so formal as previously, as though the Jaybirds were anxious to get at their task. The Beavers started Farrell at center, Farber and Jordan at guard, and Krash and Mount at forward. Don sat with Peanuts and Bud on the bench and watched for the Jaybirds' strategy to unfold.

It was simple enough. Killer Kane simply led an aroused and coherent club to new heights. They were as rough as ever. Don and Bud went into the game and were shoved around, maneuvered off balance as the score grew. The second half was no better than the first.

Bud insisted on playing although the cause grew hopeless. He needed to work out, he said. Towering, he stopped the flow of the Jaybirds almost single-handed for the final five minutes but it was far too late. The home team won 110 to 94. It was a complete rout and the Jaybirds fans raised the rafters with wild applause and renewed hopes.

The Beavers went back to the motel in the rain. The odds always favored the home team and the Jaybirds would be hot tomorrow. Don and Beans went to their room to freshen up their apparel for the late-night snack.

The phone rang and Beans answered. He said, "Oh, hey! Yeah . . . how are you? Well . . . uh . . . no, don't come over here . . . Yeah, I'll get a cab . . . see you . . ."

He hung up, cocked an eye at Don and dialed the room number of Martha and Alicia. He said, "Hey, hon, guy just called me . . . old college chum. I gotta see him for an hour or so . . . meet you downstairs . . . if I ain't there don't wait, hear? Love you, baby."

Don said, "Old college pal, huh, Beansy-boy?"

"Well, what's a guy to do? Supposin' she came over?"

"Doesn't she attend the games? Won't she see Alicia there?"

"Oh, no. She works for the phone company, gets off at eleven. Real nice girl, honest."

Don said, "They're all nice girls, right?"

Beans considered, adjusting a scarf at his open-neck collar. "Well, I'll tell you. Some's nicer than others. But none of them are real bad. See you later."

Don went downstairs to the coffee shop. Bud and Hobie Reed were at a table in the corner. They beckoned to him.

He said, "I'm expecting Martha, you don't mind?"

"She knows the game," said the coach dourly. "That other one, that girl of Beansy-boy's . . . nothing!"

"She's a real nice girl," Don said, thinking of Beans, out with the telephone operator on a rainy night in Northwest City, wondering at his roommate's nerve.

Bud said, "Sit down anyway. Coach has the right score. You might's well know it. Some of the guys . . . well, better let it stay among us chickens."

Reed nodded. "You've got a level head, Don. Never did see a rookie so mature in his thinking."

"But I'm still a rookie—with a broken beak."

"And willing to play."

"Yes. Anxious to play if I can do any good."

Bud said, "It's tomorrow or never."

"Right," said the coach. "If they beat us tomorrow we get two days' rest—but two days won't do us any good. We're at the end of our string."

"We got to turn it on," said Bud. "All the way, man."

Don considered. "I think I see it. We're not going to get any better. You, Peanuts, or me. They win tomorrow —they've got the momentum. They have the home court. They have—Killer."

"Kane's an emotional player," said Reed. "And he can bring up the others. Give them tomorrow's game and we're done for."

"It's too much for a rookie," Bud said. "But like coach says, you're not a run-of-the-mill greenhorn."

"I'd like to start you and Bud," said Reed. He looked around the coffee shop. "Where's Beans?"

"He had an errand," said Don, coughing. "He'll be around."

The girls were entering the room. He called them over. Martha looked at them and said, "We'll take the next table. You men want to talk."

"Do we look that solemn?" Bud Alcorn laughed. "Sit down, you pretty ones. It'll brighten the corner where we are."

"There's music to that," Martha told him. The girls sat down. Alicia was placid as usual—she believed everything Beans told her, Don thought.

Hobie Reed had circles beneath his eyes. He said, "I'll talk to the others. You understand that I know I'm asking too much of you."

"Not ever," said Bud Alcorn. He watched the coach walk across to where Krash and Farber and Charlie Mount were seated. "You never played under another coach in this league, man. You won't ever play for one a tenth so considerate."

"He's special," agreed Don. "He puts it up to you, directly."

"He suffers with you," Bud went on. "He consults with you. Man, I played for coaches that didn't even speak to you off the court. I played for men that hated me because I made more money than they did. Hobie Reed, he's something else."

"His wife and kids are darling," said Alicia. "I hope you win for their sake."

Don looked at her in surprise. "Do you know what it means to them?"

"I may not know basketball but I can count," said Alicia. "I know what it means to the married boys, too. Thirty thousand dollars. Each. Apiece."

Martha said, "College for the children. The mortgage on the house. Oh yes, we know what it means."

"And for the coach a long-time job," said Bud. "He's responsible. He's the general manager as well as the coach. If Kane beats us—well, Hobie traded Kane. Owners don't think of anything but winning, believe me."

They ate their light meal. Tomorrow's breakfast would be steak and eggs but they needed sleep, complete rest for that night. They talked awhile and Don thought again of Alcorn and what a great man he was and how fortunate a rookie could be to call this lonely giant a friend.

Later he said good night to Martha in the corridor. The parting kiss was now a custom between them. This time she clung close to him and he knew she felt the strain he was laboring beneath.

She whispered, "It's not just a game. It's a big thing, Don. I know how big it is."

"Yes. You know." He shivered. "A man only gets a few chances at something this important to so many of his friends."

"It's tomorrow night, isn't it?"

"Yes."

"That's what Pa said. He's rooting for you all the way."

"I know. The Halls . . . you're a wonderful family." He stopped. He was afraid to say more at this moment. He already had too much to think about. He kissed her again and went down to his room.

It was midnight. He undressed and prowled the room, wondering about Beans. He had to get some sleep but his brain was whirling. He turned on the television set but the talk show with the comics and the underdressed actress guest did not hold his attention.

He clicked off the set. He was worried about Beans. He walked the floor for a while, then donned his dark sweat suit and basketball shoes and let himself out of the room, unable to stand the four walls. He went through the lobby. It was deserted. He let himself out. The rain had stopped and it was cool and pleasant. He decided to jog awhile, to tire himself for sleep.

He was at the curving driveway of the motel when a taxicab drew up and the familiar figure of Beans Jordan emerged and reached for his money clip to pay the driver.

Two motorcycles roared in from the opposite direction, and the engines stalled. Two men in black-leather jackets ran quickly to Beans and the cabdriver. Don saw the gleam of the night light on shining blades.

He ran without thinking. He came in behind the dark, threatening figures. He heard the leader speak.

"Hand it over, punk. You, too, driver. Let's have it quick before we open you up a little."

Don caught the nearest one by the nape of the neck. He spun him and hit him a chop behind the jugular. As he turned he saw the cabdriver dive low at the knees of the second man. He threw a roundhouse punch to aid the parabola performed by the holdup man. He saw Beans lash out and kick the same one behind the ear.

The cabdriver said, "Hey, that was neat." He was a smiling, youthful fellow with a missing tooth. "Saved my night's take, you did."

Beans said, "You did okay your own self, there." He handed the young man another five-dollar bill. "Okay if we just leave them there?"

"All right with me," grinned the youth. "I'm a basketball fan. Wouldn't want you fellows in trouble, right?"

"Right," said Don. "And thanks."

The cabdriver looked at Beans. "Uh—you know that dame you were with when I picked you up?"

"Oh, sure. Nice girl."

"Yeah? These two birds are friends of hers."

"You're kiddin'!"

"I'm a local," said the driver. "I know these punks. They're high on pills or pot or somethin' right now. Your girl friend hangs out with this crowd."

He winked and waved and got into his cab and backed out of the driveway. Don yanked Beans out of the dim light of the driveway and into the motel. They went to their room and sat down. In a moment there was the sound of the cycles pulling away.

Don said, "Cabdrivers. You're a lucky cat, Beansy-boy."

"She seemed like a real nice girl. A big laugher. How was I to know?"

Don said coldly, "You weren't to know. You leave Alicia alone and go off with another girl. What do you care, that's the point? What do you care for anyone?"

"Oh, come on, roomie, you know how I am."

"I do. Oh, I know how you are. You're the great Beans Jordan. The miracle man. You shoot baskets. You even look as though you might learn to play the game. But you don't give one single damn for anything excepting that

Beansy-boy has a good time with the girls. Any girl, even a pot-smoking broad."

"Hey, you're on my back."

"I'm all over you," said Don. "I've gone along thinking you were just a crazy kid. Now we've got the biggest game we may ever play in tonight—and you're out cattin' around and damned near getting yourself stabbed. Oh, you're a dandy, all right."

"Nothin' happened. You were on the spot like always."

"Like always? Like for the last time, Beansy-boy," Don said in disgust. "The very last time. Win, lose, or draw tonight, that means. I'm not about to mess with a character that can have the commissioner of basketball on my neck because he hasn't got the sense of a duck."

Beans seemed about to weep. "You don't mean that, roomie. You're just soundin' off because you're sore."

"I mean it in spades," Don told him. "I mean that you've done it to me for the last time. All year long I've defended you, worked with you, thought you were a great guy if you would only wake up. So now you can keep right on sleeping. Go to bed, will you?"

Beans said, "Now, wait, Don. I mean, you're my pal."

"I'd rather be pals with an orangutan," said Don. "Or a black-widow spider. Just shut up and let me sleep, will you?"

He flung himself into bed. Anger, unlike worriment, did not keep him from slumbering. He left Beans sitting in bewilderment and pain, staring at himself in the mirror on the wall.

11

Mr. Brand arrived just before Don was to leave for the auditorium. The cabdriver was the same grinning young man of the previous night's engagement.

"See you at the game," the driver said. "Takin' the night off to see you California guys get beat."

"Look hard." Don waved to him. "How are you, father?"

"Puzzled," said Mr. Brand as they walked toward the scene of the coming contest.

"About what, sir?"

"People today. Girls."

"Girls, sir?"

"Kitty McCoy. She announced she is marrying Homer. Now I always thought Kitty was smitten with you, son."

"She's been going out with Homer for a year, off and on."

"They are business acquaintances." Mr. Brand shook his head. "I wouldn't have thought Homer appealed to Kitty."

"Father, I guess I'd better tell you something." He swallowed hard. He had not thought it through, it was just that now seemed the propitious moment.

"What is it?"

"Well, it's Martha Hall. I mean, I think I'm . . . I know I'm in love with her."

"Ah! Now I see." His father nodded, pleased with himself.

"Yes, sir?"

"Now I understand why Kitty had tears in her eyes when she told me she was going to marry Homer."

"Oh, come on, father. Kitty always called me 'Junior,' didn't take me seriously at all."

"That was before you became a professional basketball player. It has made a difference, you know."

"Yes. It made a difference in me."

His father took hold of his arm. "It made a difference to me, also, Donald. I promise. I shall never call you 'Junior' again."

They were entering the side door of the auditorium. Before Don could answer his father grinned widely at him, saluted, and hurried away to where Martha and Alicia had arranged his seating.

Don touched the plaster on his nose. Things were happening fast and furious. Kitty married . . . Beans acting like a whipped dog . . . Martha . . . he would have to speak with Martha after the game . . .

He was the last to enter the dressing room, having waited behind for his father. There was a buzz of low conversation. Hobie Reed was talking to George Farrell, emphasizing each word with a fist pounded into his palm. He was telling George how good he was, how well he could perform tonight, Don knew.

Bud was talking to cousin Charlie and the two silent ones, Farber and Krash, were listening, nodding. Beans was dressed and sitting apart from the others.

Don got into his uniform, debating with himself about Beans. When he regarded it one way the hillbilly kid was no different than he had been yesterday, a scatterbrain with talent and an ingenuous charm. On the other hand, he was a reckless individual lacking thoughtfulness for others, a would-be swinging playboy. The remaining factor was that he could drill a basketball through the hoop from anywhere within midcourt and the Beavers needed him. The question remaining was—how could his talent be used for the night?

Peanuts whispered in his ear, "Everybody on the club is high as a kite exceptin' that buddy of yours. What's with him?"

"Either guilty conscience or he's sulking."

"He just sits and stares a lot."

"Let him." Don had decided, he realized. "It's good for his soul."

"A soul brother he ain't." Peanuts grinned. "You ready, rookie?"

"Is a rookie ever ready in a spot like this?"

"Nope. But you'll do." Peanuts slapped his back and went back to talk with Beans, who sat with his head down, silent.

There was no pregame talk, no new strategy, nothing but the same old story. You ran with the tough guys and you wore them down or they wore you down. You fought Killer Kane every instant of the ball game or he rode you down and stomped on you. They all knew it, the coach knew it, there was no use in anything but facing the facts, facing that they were underdogs and hurting and the Jaybirds lusted for their life's blood—and the thirty thousand dollars that went with victory.

Don took time with his shoelaces. He took time drawing on his sweat suit. He had to build it inside, psyching himself. He was up against the toughest proposition he could ever face, starting this game, knowing how they depended upon him. He would have to find extra speed to help out Bud, as would Charlie and all the others. He would have to stay out of harm's way lest his nose be broken again and still play better than he knew how to play. He had to get himself up above his natural resources and remain that way for two halves of a bitter game. He did not detect the appealing glance of Beans as they went out for the preliminary warm-up, nor when they returned, nor when they went out to begin the game. He had wrapped himself deep in his own attempt to be ready.

Across the way Killer Kane was studying the opening lineup. Now he turned and spoke to the Jaybirds. He seemed relaxed and confident, his hands moving, always moving, opening and closing into fists. They were quick hands, hurtful hands.

Bud Alcorn said, "Okay, all the way." They touched flesh and went onto the court.

Beans Jordan sat on the bench, his shoulders hunched. He was not the cocky individual of former days. He was serious, his eyes questing, his mouth turned down. Peanuts, ever solicitous, curious, trying to be helpful, sat beside him. Hobie Reed, poised on the edge of the midway spot, tried hard not to show the concern he must feel.

At center court Moe Drabski stood with hands on knees looking meaningfully down at the elaborate contraption on Bud's knee, intimating that for once he would get the jump. The referee threw up the ball.

Bud went skyward as though he had never known an injury. He tapped the ball back to Red Farber. The Jaybirds flocked down to defend. Don instinctively looked for Kane.

There was a difference in the play of the Jaybirds. Kane was after Farber, working close, ignoring Don or anything but the bouncing ball. Don hustled to the sideline left in the direction of Beaver offensive attack. Farber was beset by two men now, the Jaybirds going all out on the press.

Farber passed to Krash but immediately the Beaver forward was covered, smothered as the defenders switched. Don ran around the ball and set a pick.

Krash fell back and shot the ball to Charlie Mount. Working on Don's pick, Mount went high and shot for the basket.

The ball dropped through. Once more the Beavers had scored the opening two points.

Now there was Kane again, bringing back the ball. The Jaybirds were racing for the basket. Don found that his rest on the bench due to his injury had given him the extra speed he needed, but Bud Alcorn could not run as of old. It was four men down against five.

Arnold scored for the Jaybirds.

Farber came with the attack and Don hit the crosscourt route. Kane was there, digging at him with the famous elbow. He spun and let Kane run over his leg. No harm, no foul, the ball was going to Krash. Bud went to the low post. Johnny passed to Alcorn. Don circled behind Charlie Mount. The pass was to him. Mount blocked out Kane.

Don made the jump shot for the second Beaver basket. He turned and ran as fast as he could. The Jaybirds knew this was the game they had to win and that winning it would give them the huge edge they wanted for the finale. They were all out, every man giving his best.

The Beavers matched them through the first quarter. They were over their heads and they knew it but they kept hammering away, always bringing the score to evens. It read twenty-five to twenty-five at the quarter. Don went to the sideline breathing very little harder than before his nose was broken despite playing without relief. Bud Alcorn sat down. George Farrell stood up, his face emotionless but his knees trembling just a little.

Hobie Reed said, "Beans, you try it. Do *not* shoot from outside, it's too close. Pass and run and run and pass."

Beans started, jumped to his feet. It seemed as though he had not expected to get into the game, as though he believed he was being punished, as though Don had put the position straight to him early that morning in their room.

The coach sat between Bud and Don and said, "Kane is terrific when he switches off. He's playing it cool tonight."

"Only one foul is plenty cool for him," said Bud.

Farrell was trying hard against Drabski but the margin between them was evident. The ball came to Beans and he had no place to go with it. He dribbled in a circle. Kane came to him and he dribbled behind his back. He wheeled with his pure grace and speed and passed to Charlie.

Mount was blocked from the lane. He feinted for the hoop. He passed off to Beans running through. Beans laid it up and in.

Bud said, "If he's hot we're all right."

But Beans could not stop Kane. The Killer dribbled all the way down the court and got the ball to Drabski. The center pivoted and shot over Farrell's head to even the score once more.

Bud said, "I'd better go back in. Drabski's way up there."

"Don, you'd better go along," said Reed. "We need the balance you and Bud give us."

Beans came off, looking at Don like a lost puppy.

Don said, "Hey, nice work."

"Gee, thanks . . . Kane's wingin' it, roomie," said Beans eagerly. "He's really wingin' it."

Don went into the swarm of the game. "Wingin' it," meant Kane was soloing in the patois of Beans Jordan and Beans should know. It meant Kane was free-lancing, not playing in the tight format of the Jaybirds' usual patterns. Don tried to study it as he ran.

It was a race all the way. That was the overall scheme of the game. The Jaybirds, without serious injuries, with what they thought were stronger reserves, would try and run the Beavers into exhaustion, then beat them in the last moments of play. And Kane was winging it.

Beans was correct. The all-star Kane was taking more than his share of the responsibility. The Jaybirds all ran and passed and were sure-handed. They were almost without turnovers as the half dwindled down to a few seconds.

Farber had the ball with the score fifty to fifty. Kane came in at him. Don tried to get in the way. Kane bowled him over. It was not called a foul since Don had, apparently inadvertently, put a block on Killer. It was Drabski who stole the ball and passed to Kane. The Jaybird leader shot as the clock ran out. From twenty-five feet out he hit the rim. The ball rolled, hesitated, then dropped in. Kane let out an exultant yell and thrust a clenched fist toward the ceiling.

It seemed like little, a two-point lead going to the locker rooms for the intermission between halves. But it meant a lot to basketball pros. It meant that this was what Kane wanted, what he was fighting for. The edge, two points, one point—anything to win. It meant the Jaybirds had showed their strength in the final seconds of the half. It meant they would come rushing out with that all-important momentum to begin the second half.

Reed said to the team, "You know why Kane made that last bucket?"

"I didn't cover him," said Don.

"Nobody is covering him. Somebody must."

"Me," said Don.

"Yes," said the coach. "But without breaking our offensive play. You understand?"

"Yes," said Don. His nose was hurting a little. He buried his face in a cold towel. When he looked up Beans was standing over him.

Beans said, "I can help."

"Sure," Don told him. "You saw what he was doing before I did."

"Uh—you're not sore at me any more?"

Don took a deep breath. "No. I'm not sore at you."

"I know you're right. I thought about it all night. And this morning. It never struck me before. Fun. I was always havin' fun. This ain't fun, this game."

"It's a certain kind of fun."

"If we win, it's fun. If we lose, all these guys will die a little. I thought about it."

Don said, "Okay, Beans."

"You sure?"

"I'm sure."

"Then we'll do what Hobie says."

"Yes. We'll do what Hobie says."

They went back onto the court, Don and Bud in the game, Beans on the bench. They plunged into the maelstrom which they knew they must dominate.

In the beginning Kane had tried to dominate him, Don realized. The personal antagonism had been there but beneath it was the determination of the veteran to intimidate the rookie and render him valueless. Now it was the time for Don to go after his tormentor.

He brought all the experience gained through the long pro season to the task. From the tipoff he was on Killer's trail. They raged up and down the court in an individual battle when the Jaybirds were on the offense.

When the Beavers had the ball it was Kane's turn, but he had set up a way to go and the other Jaybirds still went man for man. It ran even all the way. At the end of the third quarter the score was sixty-nine for the Jaybirds, sixty-seven for the Beavers.

Bud let the sweat run from his chin. "Remember when

we were kids and it was tight and we always came up with some big play? Some smart strategy?"

"That's what we thought," said Don.

"No way." The big center sighed. "My knee is about ready to go."

"I can see it," said Hobie Reed. He was pale with the strain. "We'll go without you."

"Not nearly," said Bud. "It hasn't gone, not yet."

Beans was harassing Kane. There were three quick fouls in succession. The score remained two points in the favor of the Jaybirds. It seemed like a hundred points.

"Time's a-wasting," said Bud, standing up, trying not to show the pain he felt.

"All right," said Hobie Reed. "Don."

Kane scored again to make it eighty-eight to eighty-four, a well-defended, low-scoring game for two championship teams. Don followed Bud onto the floor. Beans slapped his palm as they passed and sadly shook his head. There were forty seconds to play, which seemed no time at all but in this game was time enough.

Bud said, "Zone press, double time."

It was the only way. Kane was now slowing it down, talking to his men. They needed only to hold the ball.

Don caught the Killer at midcourt and committed the intentional foul. Kane went to the line. He was not laughing. His face was grim. He bounced the ball. He set himself. He lofted it for the basket.

The shot seemed to go inside the hoop. Then it did a reverse spin. Then it dropped into the hands of Charlie Mount.

Don was already running. Mount flung the ball with all his considerable strength. Kane had turned and was racing. Arnold went for the ball. Don leaped. He stretched his arms.

The ball felt good in his hands. He hit the floor running. He jumped and shot. The basket trembled but the ball went through the quivering net. It was eighty-eight to eighty-six.

Again Kane had to control the play. Don slid in close. Kane snarled and slung an elbow. Don sucked in his middle and slapped. The ball broke loose. Bud left his feet and slid along the floor to prevent it going out of bounds and being turned back to the Jaybirds. He got his fingers on it. He flipped it to Farber.

Farber dribbled. The Jaybirds had to defend and be careful of a foul. Farber managed to wrench loose and Don came tin-canning away from Kane. The other Beavers were covered. Farber passed to Don.

Again it was a quick jump shot. Don tossed it for the brass ring and it counted.

The scoreboard flickered and the figures read eighty-eight points for each team. The Jaybirds took a time out.

Bud limped to the bench. "That slide for home did it. There's no more left in the old man. I'd louse it up."

Hobie Reed said, "I know . . . okay . . . Jordan."

Beans came up like a jack-in-the-box. "Me?"

"You. We want speed and we want a basket. We want everything going faster than before. I don't care how you do it. Just get me that score." His eyes were on the clock.

It was the Jaybirds from under the basket. They could go into overtime, and they were at full strength. Kane was staring at Bud on the bench and there was triumph in his eyes. He could hold the ball for twenty-three seconds, take the shot. If he missed it was still a tie and into the extra period. When he saw Beans and Don come on without Bud he laughed and motioned to Moe Drabski to take advantage of the mismatch, to handle the smaller players.

Kane took the throw-in. He began his dribble, no slower, no faster than before. He brought it over the black line. He looked for his open man.

Moving with blinding speed, Don and Beans converged. They were upon the Killer before he knew they were in the neighborhood. They encompassed him with four arms waving and seeking and probing. He turned and they turned with him. He sought to pass and they prevented him while the other Beavers zone-pressed their men.

Kane was a superstar but he was not as young as the two who assailed him. He made his move. The clock was making its last half round of the game. It was Don who had the last chance.

He stuck in his hand. The sound of palm on leather was clean. An official was leaning in watching. The ball broke loose. Kane went for it. Don went for it.

They came together. Beans stole the ball.

Down the court Farber was waving. Beans threw to him. Johnny Krash was beneath the hoop. The pass went to Krash. The solid, quiet little forward dropped it into the basket as easy as though he were shooting fish in a barrel.

The klaxon sounded a long, mournful note for the home crowd. The game was over. The crippled underdog team from Canyon City had won the world championship.

There was little sound except for the yells of joy from the Beavers and the shrill voices of Martha and Alicia in the grandstand. They went in a tight group, every man touching the other, to the dressing room where Hobie Reed was mobbed and held from them by the newspapermen and the television and radio people. The others escaped into the dressing room and barred the door and threw themselves upon one another and acted like little kids on a Sunday picnic.

By the time the coach got to them they were settled down to thorough enjoyment. Beans was babbling, "I passed to Red . . . I passed to him. I saw the lane, I could've taken it in. All on account of you, roomie, I passed to him."

"You could have scored," Hobie Reed told him. "I saw that you had time. I thought you were going to do it."

Beans became solemn. "So help me, coach. I promise. Never again. I grew up since last night. When I thought my roomie was real mad at me . . . I couldn't handle it, honest. Next year—you'll see. I promise."

Bud draped a long, heavy arm about the shoulders of the two youngest Beavers. "You cats, I'll be ready for another year, too. I can't quit now. What the coach and these kids have done is start a dynasty. You know? A dynasty of champs, you dudes."

Hobie Reed said, "Not without you, big man . . . the champagne is on Mr. Brand again . . . back at the motel."

Martha was pretty in a new outfit. They were out at poolside. It was beginning to rain again but they did not notice. The party was going on inside.

Don said, "I already told father."

She nestled closer. "Pa already told me."

"He what?"

"He said if I didn't grab you off he'd never forgive me. We never had a real championship player in the family."

They kissed again.

Then Don asked, "What about Alicia and Beans?"

"She has an offer to do a really good movie. She's not as dumb as people think."

"You mean she's giving him up?"

"Oh, no," said Martha. "That's what I say. She's going to stick around and have fun and see how he turns out."

Don said, "That Beans."

"You think he'll show for the wedding?"

"Oh, he'll be my best man." Don reflected. "But it's an even bet he'll be late."

He kissed her again. It was a nice habit to get into, he had learned.

ABOUT THE AUTHOR

WILLIAM R. COX's interest in sports began when he was four years old and his father presented him with boxing gloves, a baseball and a bat. He played baseball through high school and on semipro teams, often covering the games in which he played for the Newark *Sunday Call*.

His family was in the ice, coal and wood business, and he says that from hauling, lifting and shoveling he developed muscles "coming out of my ears . . ." But, realizing that a writer can't live by sports alone, Mr. Cox began writing crime novels and westerns. Only recently has he returned to the sports scene for his themes.

Mr. Cox has written thirteen sports juveniles, including *Five Were Chosen, The Contender, Chicano Cruz,* and *PLAYOFF*.

Don't wait until tomorrow!

SEND FOR YOUR FREE BANTAM BESTSELLERS CATALOG TODAY!

It lists hundreds of money-saving bestsellers originally priced from $3.75 to $15.00—bestsellers that are yours now for as little as 60¢ to $1.95!

The catalog gives you a great opportunity to get the books you missed, while it also helps you build your own private library at huge savings.

So don't delay any longer—send for your catalog TODAY! It's absolutely FREE!

Just send us a post card with the Information below or use this handy coupon:

BANTAM BOOKS, INC.
Dept. FC, 414 East Golf Road, Des Plaines, Ill. 60016

I'm tired of paying high prices for good books. Please send me your latest free catalog of Bantam Books.

Name_____

Address_____

City_____ State_____ Zip Code_____

Please allow up to three weeks for delivery.

FC—10/72

PSYCHIC WORLD

Here are some of the leading books that delve into the world of the occult—that shed light on the powers of prophecy, of reincarnation and of foretelling the future.

- [ ] **THE SEARCH FOR THE GIRL WITH THE BLUE EYES** by Jess Stearn. The story of a young woman's reincarnation. (N4591—95¢)

- [ ] **PSYCHIC PEOPLE** by Eleanor Touhey Smith. The revealing account of 19 men and women with strange and supernatural powers. (N4471—95¢)

- [ ] **EDGAR CAYCE: THE SLEEPING PROPHET** by Jess Stearn. The bestselling study of the late mystic's prophecies and astounding readings. (Q6764—$1.25)

- [ ] **A GIFT OF PROPHECY** by Ruth Montgomery. The phenomenal account of Jeane Dixon's uncanny ability to forsee the future. (N4223—95¢)

- [ ] **YOGA, YOUTH AND REINCARNATION** by Jess Stearn describes the skeptical author's experience with the ancient art of yoga. (Q6508—$1.25)

- [ ] **THE COMPLETE BOOK OF PALMISTRY** by Joyce Wilson. A step-by-step fully-illustrated course in the ancient art of reading palms. (P5689—$1.00)

- [ ] **PSYCHIC DISCOVERIES BEHIND THE IRON CURTAIN** by Sheila Ostrander & Lynn Schroeder. Reports of government sponsored research on artificial reincarnation, astrological birth control and other psychic phenomena. Fully documented discoveries. (Q6581—$1.25)

Ask for them at your local bookseller or use this handy coupon:

Bantam Books, Inc., Dept. PW, 666 Fifth Ave., New York, N. Y. 10019

Please send me the Bantam Books which I have checked. I am enclosing $_____ (check or money order—no currency or C.O.D.'s Please). Note: Please include 10¢ per book for postage and handling on orders of less than six books.

Name_____

Address_____

City_____State_____Zip Code_____

Please allow about four weeks for delivery. PW—5/72
This offer expires 5/73.

Facts at Your Fingertips!

☐ **MOVIES ON TV.** Stars, stories and ratings to over 7000 movies now being shown on television. (T7004—$1.50)

☐ **THE THORNDIKE BARNHART HANDY DICTIONARY.** The latest revised edition with 36,000 entries plus tables of weight, grammar, etc. (S6594—75¢)

☐ **DICTIONARY OF CLASSICAL MYTHOLOGY.** Over 2000 full, concise descriptions of Greek and Roman myths, heroes, authors, works, places and symbols. (NM4288—95¢)

☐ **AMY VANDERBILT'S EVERYDAY ETIQUETTE.** America's foremost authority offers up-to-date advice on correct behavior in any situation. (Q5666—$1.25)

☐ **SOULE'S DICTIONARY OF ENGLISH SYNONYMS.** 20,000 entries with colloquial expressions, notes on technical words and clarifications of usage. (NN4783—95¢)

☐ **THE POOR MAN'S GUIDE TO ANTIQUE COLLECTING.** Advice from an expert about how to avoid the pitfalls and find the treasures. (RR5854—$1.45)

☐ **ANYONE CAN GO TO COLLEGE.** A guidebook to 100's of large, small and medium-sized U.S. colleges. (P7264—$1.00)

☐ **A DICTIONARY OF SYMPTOMS** by Dr. Joan Gomez. (Y5754—$1.95)

☐ **CONSUMER BEWARE.** One of the most comprehensive books to help all shoppers get the most for their money. (Y7484—$1.95)

Ask for them at your local bookseller or use this handy coupon:

Bantam Books, Inc., Dept. RB, Room 2450,
666 Fifth Avenue, N. Y., N. Y. 10019

Please send me the titles I have checked.

Name_____

Address_____

City_____State_____Zip Code_____

(Please send check or money order. No currency or C.O.D.'s. Add 10¢ per book on orders of less than 5 books to cover the cost of postage and handling.) Please allow about four weeks for delivery.

RB—10/72

Louis L'Amour
America's Fastest-Selling Western Writer

One of the top writers of western stories, his power-packed tales are exciting reading.

- [ ] BRIONNE — S7037 — 75¢
- [ ] THE LONELY MEN — S6752 — 75¢
- [ ] MUSTANG MAN — S6781 — 75¢
- [ ] THE SACKETT BRAND — S6762 — 75¢
- [ ] THE EMPTY LAND — S6745 — 75¢
- [ ] DARK CANYON — S7042 — 75¢
- [ ] RADIGAN — S7013 — 75¢
- [ ] CATLOW — S7174 — 75¢
- [ ] FALLON — S7145 — 75¢
- [ ] LANDO — S6996 — 75¢
- [ ] THE BURNING HILLS — S5797 — 75¢
- [ ] HIGH LONESOME — S7048 — 75¢
- [ ] SILVER CANYON — S6759 — 75¢
- [ ] KILLOE — S7085 — 75¢
- [ ] FLINT — S6746 — 75¢
- [ ] SACKETT — S6748 — 75¢
- [ ] BROKEN GUN — S6749 — 75¢
- [ ] THE DAY BREAKERS — S7060 — 75¢
- [ ] TAGGART — S6528 — 75¢
- [ ] NORTH TO THE RAILS — S5747 — 75¢
- [ ] UNDER THE SWEETWATER RIM — S5911 — 75¢

Ask for them at your local bookseller or use this handy coupon:

BANTAM BOOKS, INC., Dept. LL, Room 2450,
666 Fifth Ave., New York, N. Y. 10019

Please send me the titles I have indicated.

Name_____

Address_____

City_____State_____Zip Code_____

(Please send check or money order. No currency or C.O.D.'s. Add 10¢ per book on orders of less than 5 books to cover the cost of postage and handling.)

Please allow about four weeks for delivery.   LL—1/72

"HITLER'S WAR"

From the German point of view and secret Nazi documents never before revealed to the public, here is the whole gigantic drama of the most crucial days of World War II. Bantam now presents six books that individually capture the major personalities and events of the war.

- [ ] **THE LAST 100 DAYS** by John Toland Incredible episodes never before revealed! The tumultuous and bestselling account of the final days of World War II. D5812/$1.65

- [ ] **HITLER & NAZISM** A portrait of the man and how he infected a whole nation with his twisted madness! S5937/75¢

- [ ] **THE BLACK MARCH** The personal story of an SS man. The brutal truth behind Hitler's school for atrocity! N5857/95¢

- [ ] **THE PICTORIAL HISTORY OF THE THIRD REICH** A nightmarish rogues' gallery of Nazi infamy, including portraits of Hitler, Himmler, Goebbels and Goering. Q6705/$1.25

- [ ] **HITLER'S PLOT TO KILL THE BIG THREE** One of the most exciting and unbelievable documents to come out of World War II—chronicling Hitler's desperate plan to kill Roosevelt, Churchill and Stalin! N5371/95¢

Buy them at your local bookstore or use this handy coupon:

Bantam Books, Inc., Dept. HW, Room 2450, 666 Fifth Ave., New York, N. Y. 10019

Please mail me the Bantam Best-sellers checked above. I am enclosing $_____(Check or money order—no currency, no C.O.D.'s please. If less than 5 books, add 10¢ per book for postage and handling.)

Name_____

Address_____

City_____State_____Zip Code_____

Please allow about three weeks for delivery. HW—9/72